SO YOUR BIGGEST FAN IS A BODY SNATCHER

POST-APOCALYPTIC DJ: BOOK 1

K.C. CORDELL

You obviously have highly discerning taste...

And if this weirdness is right up your alley, then you should definitely sign up to receive updates on upcoming books, behind-the-scene sneak peeks, and various chitchat from the author.

www.kccordell.com/newsletter

For Ringu. You are the wind beneath my wings.

1

"WHAT THE HELL is wrong with you, Sebastian?" Meza grumbles over the roaring engine, pounding hooves, and yelling townsfolk. Sizzling blaster fire glows against the rapidly dimming sky.

"They started it!" Sebastian Yun puts pedal to the metal for all it's worth, but the mob screaming for his blood does an admirable job of keeping up despite the disparity in transportation modes.

In theory, horses should not be able to outpace a hover vehicle. But Her Royal Majesty, Sebastian's completely decked-out double-decker bus, is big and heavy. She was rebuilt to withstand monster assaults, not to win races.

Besides, it's not as if the parts Sebastian salvaged and pieced together to get HRM up and running were in the best condition to start with. Push the bus too hard and any of the many ancient parts keeping her going might just up and scream, "Screw this shit!" and depart for hoverbus-parts heaven.

Thus, he doesn't "put pedal to the metal for all it's worth" so much as put pedal to the metal as much as he dares while banking on the mob's horses tiring out very soon and quickly falling behind.

Meza pins him with a glare. It's almost as if she doubts his claim that this is all the townsfolk's fault.

"I did it for the children!" he says. "You know how kids are forced to live in them sorts of places? And you expected me to sit there and do nothing about that level of neglect? I am sorry, Meza, but that just ain't how I'm built."

"Right." With a roll of her eyes, Meza lowers the window. The clamor of the mob grows even louder.

The whooshing wind buffets against her halo of dark, textured hair as she props herself partly through the open passenger window. She grips the frame to steady herself with one hand while the other points her NX-84 Waster toward the back of HRM, where the horde of angry men and women on horseback ride like hell to keep up.

Face as placid as the moon, she fires a few shots. Warnings, that's all. A little something to make it clear that if the mob doesn't back down, she and Sebastian will defend themselves.

The message fails to land.

Return blasts light up the barren, darkening landscape in sporadic flashes. The armored bus shakes from the impact of a larger weapon but otherwise keeps on trucking.

Pun intended.

Fortunately, riding horseback and shooting accurately go together like Black Sabbath and tea parties. The sizzling blasts sail harmlessly past Meza. Hanging out the window with her own weapon drawn and lit by the blazing flashes, she looks like some kind of badass road warrior goddess.

Only a year younger than Sebastian, Meza is seventeen with a petite frame that borders on pixie. Not that he'd ever use that word to describe her. There's nothing sprite-like about her. For one thing, a cute little sprite sidekick would know how to have fun from time to time. In the handful of months they've known each other, Sebastian has yet to see her smile.

"I know you don't much like kids and all," he says, "but even you musta felt at least a little teeny, tiny ounce of pity for them."

"They were perfectly fine." She slips back into her seat and raises the passenger-side window.

"Perfectly—" He sputters, unable to believe that she would utter such flippant and callous words after witnessing that severely depraved situation with her own two peepers. He pushes unruly strands of black hair out of his eyes. Takes a breath. Prays for patience. "Meza. They ain't never heard any NWA ever. No Bone Thugs or Snoop. No Tupac!"

"Just couldn't help yourself."

"That's only West Coast '90s rap!" Sebastian says, to emphasize his point.

"It's called impulse control," she says, to reiterate hers.

He flicks his wrist to activate his data cuff. A round holo-interface pops up. Stabbing at a series of icons pulls up the feed from the camera embedded in the back of the bus. Cameras are not an easy get in the scavenging game, but at times like these, Sebastian is really glad he'd gone through the trouble.

The mob is still right on HRM's tail. They're a frantic knot of wild-eyed, frothing horses, angry-faced, shouting humans, and colorfully strobing blaster fire. All of it wrapped in an enormous dust cloud.

"They cannot still be keeping up," Sebastian says despite all evidence to the contrary. "What're they feeding them horses? Other horses? The hatred from the blackest parts of their shriveled hearts?"

"They're motivated. Far as they're concerned, you done doomed them all."

"'Cuz they heard a little music? Do they really not know how ridiculous they are?"

"More than that to them, and you know it."

"Barf! Anti-Techers. Literally the worst people in the Midlands. And, yes, that includes bandits and them idiots in the Congregation of Hope."

Although, to be fair, the average Midlander isn't overly trusting of tech. For some reason, computery stuff being the catalyst in the downfall of humanity doesn't sit well with a lot of people, even all these generations later. Go figure. As a result, most folks hadn't heard much Old World music before Sebastian started broadcasting a radio show that introduced all who would listen to delights from centuries long past. But this situation is different. These people are different.

"Ain't your place to judge what they believe," Meza says. "Just like it ain't your place to blast 'Hail Mary' at top volume from every corner of their town."

"Heh. Classic."

"Ain't laughing."

"What's new?" Sebastian asks. "Come on, even you gotta admit that was epic. Wish I coulda been inside their walls to see the look on that jerk of a town leader's face. She already looked like a professional salt sucker. Bet her whole face mighta caved in on itself."

"And that was worth all of this?" She waves a hand toward her window. Flashes of blue blaster fire brighten the dimming landscape.

"Don't you worry. They ain't catching us."

"Still leaves us on the road at night."

"Right… That."

"Right. That."

Admittedly, they are quickly approaching the wrong side of dusk, and the sky grows darker every second.

The evening hours are for shuttering windows and doors against all the things that go bump in the night. Not racing down the road attracting the attention of said night things with a bunch of noise and flashing lights.

Everybody knows this.

Everybody but the nutjobs riding furiously behind HRM.

Anti-Techers really are the worst.

"I did it for the fans!" Sebastian says. "You know I'd march into death itself for my adoring public."

"Ain't nobody in that town knew who you were."

He tosses her a lopsided grin. "They do now."

"Will you look so pleased when you're a corpse?"

Sebastian thinks about it for a few seconds. Really pictures it. "I genuinely hope so."

"For once can't you—"

"What? Be less awesome? I reckon that's like trying to contain a force of nature. Might as well ask the sun to stop shining."

She watches him, her lips drawn in a disapproving line.

His grin widens.

"Just drive." Turning away, she fixes her gaze on the graying horizon passing outside her window.

Whatever. Brooding is her default setting.

In the rear camera feed, the thunderous, yelling dust cloud is still shooting to kill, but the horses are finally starting to fall behind.

Sebastian lets out a relieved breath. Not that he was worried.

With a few flicks of his fingers, he turns on his data cuff's mic and hits the broadcast button, sending his voice out to receivers across the Midlands.

"My dear, loyal listeners, for whom I do all that I do, my people, my reason for waking every single morning. Do I ever have a tale for you!

"On this evening's installment of *So You Survived the End of the World,* a thrilling account of how I, your clever, dashing, ever-so-humble host, Sebastian Yun, smuggled a whole cache of data rings into a town that despises tech. This despite the fact that they refused to let me in. What happened after that, my fellow post-apocalyptizens, well—"

"You coulda got us killed." Meza's back is still to him. In the dusty window's faded reflection, her eyes are obscured by a black shadow, unreadable.

"In case you ain't noticed, neither of us is dead. We totally got away."

That last part is, technically, not one hundred percent true. Yet. Their pursuers haven't completely faded from the rear feed, but he, Meza, and HRM are as good as scot-free. No way those horses are catching up. Tech for the win.

"Night is young," Meza says, "and we're out in the middle of it."

"We'll be fine."

"You wouldn't do anything different. Given the chance." She turns to him at last and watches him, steady. Expectant.

She hadn't phrased that as a question, but why does this moment feel like a test? It's like she wants something from him but won't say exactly what.

It's all very un-Meza, whose usual straightforwardness has all the soft edges of a porcupine and who has gone out of her way to make it abundantly clear from the beginning that she needs absolutely nothing from him. Even her quiet expression edges into unfamiliar territory. Somewhere almost unguarded.

In her eerie earnestness, Sebastian squirms. Her unwavering stare cuts through him like cold steel. Good thing he has a legitimate excuse to look away. Eyes on the road and all that.

He remembers with a jolt that he's still broadcasting.

"Wha-what was that?" he says to his unseen audience. "I agree, listeners. Meza's acting really weird. I suspect she's been body snatched by one of them slimy sludges. You'd tell me if you were a sludgebrain, right, Meza? I mean, it's the decent thing to do.

"Well, Miss Body-Snatched Version of Meza. If you're gonna sit there and pretend to be my traveling companion, best get yourself up to speed on the ruling philosophy in this here bus.

"We're all gonna die. And in this screwed-up, monster-infested world, it's gonna happen sooner than any of us want. So what? Can't let the fear of something little like death keep you from living.

"Maybe we go out doing something epic. But our legend will live on. My listeners will share our tale far and wide. I command it. So shall it be."

Meza rises from her seat. Her eyes fall on him, and he has the odd sense that she's seeing him for the very first time. Really seeing him. And she doesn't like the view.

With a shake of her head, she starts down HRM's narrow aisle. Away from him.

"What am I doing here?"

She says it quietly. He can't be sure she meant for him to hear—or that she cares that he did.

"What?" he asks.

She continues on without another word.

"You're talking like you got an eye on the exit," he calls over his shoulder.

Still, she says nothing.

"Are you eyeing the exit?"

More silence.

For the record, Sebastian has absolutely no problem with her leaving, if that's what she wants. Meza doesn't owe him anything. No more than he owes her.

They haven't even known each other all that long. Has it even been five months? No, closer to six.

That can't be right. It feels like they've known each other longer.

Midland time. That's all it is. A day can feel like a lifetime when you're in constant survival mode. Five-almost-six months can add up to a lot of lifetimes. Maybe even an eternity.

Sebastian internally scoffs at his melodramatic train of thought. He got along just peachy before Meza came scowling into his life. He'll get along fine and dandy without her.

So she's ready to pack her bags. Why does she have to act so freakin' weird about it?

Not like he ever thought their arrangement would last forever. He's smarter than that. In fact, maybe he'll get a new companion every few months. Worked for the Doctor.

"Hey, Midlanders," Sebastian says. "Let's talk upside of knowing everybody in this world is hurtling toward an early demise. You learn pretty darn early in life not to get attached. Once you master that handy, dandy skill of detachment, nothing gets under your skin. Grandpappy got carried off by a sludgebrain? No biggie. Little Suzie ended up as some hellion's appetizer? Just another Tuesday. That guy Gary disappeared one day and you'll never know what happened to him? Congrats! You ain't gotta make good on that IOU. And—"

A rattling *BOOM* shakes HRM. The reverberations jolt Sebastian down to his bones.

"What was that?" Sebastian shouts.

Meza reappears at his side. Leaning over the console, she zooms in on the image of the rear camera feed. The mob has fallen back significantly and is no longer in pursuit, but they aim something at HRM.

"Eradicator," Meza says calmly.

"A rocket launcher! That's pretty serious tech, you pack of deranged hypocrites. These people got no principles. Oh, yeah, forgot to mention, dear listeners, yours truly is currently being chased by a bunch of Anti-Techers. You know how it goes. And I got a question. Call in if you know the answer. How'd a bunch of Anti-Techers get their hands on an Eradicator? You know how hard it is to find one of those? I do. Not that I'm jealous or anything."

"That was a miss," Meza says. "Bus won't take a direct hit from something like that."

"Not with that attitude she won't."

Meza, predictably, is not amused.

"We just gotta move outta range of that thing," he says.

Meza drops back down into the passenger seat. "They won't have line of sight once we get around that bend."

Sebastian accelerates, knowing that HRM is already giving it all she's got.

"C'mon, your majesty," he coos. "I believe in you, Mama. Don't blow out! Don't blow out! Don't blow out!"

HRM swings around the curving wall of rock.

"Yes! Yes! No—" Sebastian slams on the brakes. Then stares ahead for a full three seconds that they may or may not be able to afford. "Well, that's just annoying."

Meza gives him a glance that all but accuses him of what lies before them. But honestly, if he had the magical ability to shape the landscape, this is not what they'd be looking at.

Through the window, the road that dips into a valley is already shrouded in shadow.

The road itself becomes a simple, not especially high trestle bridge. On one side, it hugs an ordinary stony hillside. But the opposite side of the bridge dips into a valley where tall, dark shapes extend up from the ground like trees. Except that they have no branches, no leaves. And they're humongous. The last rays of the setting sun kiss the peaks of these strange rock formations.

"Who came up with the genius plan to carve a road through there?" Sebastian says.

"Bad enough to travel at night. Traveling at night through a place like that…" Meza's hand drifts to the sixteen-inch FT-M Devastator holstered against her thigh.

"Sorry, listeners," Sebastian says. "I gotta deal with a thing. Here's a bit of music to distract you from fretting over me and Meza. Worry about Stan and his poor, tragic girl-friend instead. This is Slim Shady."

Sebastian taps a button to start the selected playlist, then dismisses the holo-interface with a flick of his wrist.

Meza shakes her head. "We can't go down there."

"Is it better to let the Anti-Techers catch up to us with their rocket launcher of hypocrisy? Are you especially eager to see what that thing does up close?"

"If we turn back—"

"We might get a whole five seconds to regret that deci-sion," Sebastian says.

"Don't like either option."

"I ain't a huge fan myself."

"Know what we're facing back that way. Anything could be down there." She glares at the valley ahead. "Wouldn't even see them coming."

"Or nothing is down there, as opposed to back the way we came. Where we know we're as good as dead."

Sebastian juts a fist toward her. She eyes the hand hanging between them skeptically.

"I win, we go through," he says, "and it'll probably be fine 'cuz I bet there ain't nothing to be worried about and we'll make it to the other side with no problems. You win, we take our chances with the bloodthirsty mob, who will definitely rip us to shreds the very first chance they get."

Meza regards him flatly for another moment, then sticks out her fist. Sebastian knew she would. Because, even with her making everything suddenly weird between them, she understands there's only one way to make a decision this big.

"Rock, dagger, blaster," Sebastian chants.

She throws out blaster, her fingers forming the shape of a pistol. Sebastian's rock wins. Somehow.

He's fully aware that in real life, the person with a blaster would probably win against someone with a rock. But the rules of the game are the rules of the game.

"This game is dumb."

"Don't be a sore loser, Meza." For once, Sebastian doesn't gloat. This doesn't feel like a victory.

She scowls. "Two out of three."

Another bone-shaking *BOOM* rattles HRM. Way too close behind them, the ground explodes into a shower of rocks. Only thing that saves them from a fine future as smithereens is the fact that the Anti-Techers are shooting blind.

"Onward it is!" Sebastian declares and floors it.

Eyes glued on the tall rock formations, Meza's grimmer than usual as Sebastian guides HRM down the road. Even Sebastian, for once, keeps his mouth shut.

For a while.

"What're the chances they'll follow us?" Sebastian asks, breaking the tense silence.

"Only a moron would willingly ride through a place like this when it's nearly dark out."

"So… pretty high."

But the Anti-Techers prove they have some iota of sense. They don't follow. Which isn't as much of a relief as Sebastian thought it would be. According to the copious hours of horror movies he's consumed, when the locals steer clear of an area, it's never a good sign for witless passers through.

As HRM barrels across the bridge, the formations grow more and more massive. They're even taller than they appeared to be from a distance. The ground slopes away from the bridge, putting the bases of the formations far below.

Some spires of rock are as broad as three or four big men standing side by side, others as wide as HRM is tall. A few of the skinnier ones are more bulbous at the top, like all it would take is a good breeze to send the bulky chunk crashing down.

Picking up speed, Sebastian strokes HRM's steering wheel. "Don't be mad, my liege. I know I already done asked a lot of you tonight, but you got this. I'll give you a nice, long pampering when you're on the other side. De-rust your steps, oil all your joints, give your fans a real nice rubdown and everything."

CLA-THUNK!

"Whoa," Sebastian says.

The sound had come from beneath HRM, accompanied by a less-than-comforting shudder from the entire bus.

CA-LUNKATHUNK.

"Whoa!"

The wheel yanks free of Sebastian's control. The bus veers wildly toward the open edge of the bridge. Sebastian tugs hard on the wheel, spinning the vehicle back toward the road. It's an overcorrection. The bus careens toward the stony, hillside wall.

He slams his foot down on the brake.

HRM's momentum laughs at his attempt to prevent disaster. The bus doesn't merely slam into the rocky cliffside. It barrels and bounces up a modest grouping of roadside boulders as if going after a rock-climbing world record.

Then the current of air that keeps HRM sailing over all obstacles cuts out.

The bus remembers gravity is a thing and unceremoniously drops the foot and a half that usually stands between its undercarriage and the ground. It screeches backward for a heart-jolting second before coming to a stop at a weird angle, tilted upward and listing slightly.

For a moment, Sebastian doesn't dare breathe.

He takes stock of the situation and confirms that, no, he is not, in fact, dead. Only then does he let out a shaky breath and unclench his jaw. His grip on the wheel is so tight Meza might have to peel his fingers from it.

Sebastian stabs the engine button.

The bus chokes and trembles. A painful, metallic, whining noise comes from somewhere below them. It all but confirms what the blinking dashboard lights scream at him.

They're stuck.

On a middle-of-nowhere road.

With night fast approaching.

2

HRM AGAIN MAKES that unholy screeching-grinding sound when Sebastian attempts to start the engine one more time. He stops almost immediately. He hates hearing her in pain.

He'd rebuilt Her Royal Majesty bit by bit, piece by piece, with his own two hands—and maybe eventually with a little help from Meza, but only after he'd done most of the heavy lifting. The point is Sebastian can diagnose the former band tour bus's ailments from sound and feel alone.

"That's the—"

"Forward-left current generator. Airflow regulator's offline." She already has a diagnostic screen pulled up on the holo-interface of her data cuff.

An airflow regulator is one of those diva parts. If it's not happy, nobody else is either.

"I offer you my sincerest apologies, my liege." Sebastian gives HRM's steering wheel a comforting caress. "I done pushed you too hard, didn't I?"

Thanks to the angle at which the bus has crashed, gravity tugs at him in a lopsided kind of way, lightly pressing him against the back of his seat. On the other side of the windshield and Sebastian's window, the view is nothing but a wall of striped orange rock glowing in the bright beams of HRM's headlights.

"Ain't going nowhere like this." Meza's frown deepens as she zooms in on the red, blinking section of the bus's schematics. "Just did a full maintenance on all the CGens. Shouldna crapped out so soon."

"You wanna be awesome and tell me you got some magical way of fixing it from the inside?"

Meza cuts him a flat look.

"I didn't think so."

Giving up on starting the engine, he flicks the control to lower the parking legs. Then winces at the resulting keening of metal against rocks.

"The parking legs won't fully extend," Sebastian says, hardly surprised. "The front ones are hitting against them rocks. There's no way we're getting the protective skirt down."

He shivers, recalling horror stories of monsters slithering underneath vehicles during the long night. A real fun surprise for the unsuspecting human who steps out in the morning, or crawls underneath to do some repairs.

There's a reason protective skirts became standard. It's the same reason lowering them when at a stop is as automatic as reaching for a blaster at the first sight of claws or fangs.

But even if the parking legs and protective skirt could fully extend right now, it wouldn't be a ton of help. The way the front of the bus is propped up on those boulders, anything could get cozy under HRM during the night.

Through Meza's window, the graying dusk has already tipped toward an unsettling umber. They're losing light fast. Even faster now that the sun is blocked by all of these looming rock formations.

Beyond the bridge, the spaces between the stony behemoths play host to inky shadows. Nightmares lurk in shadows like that.

"Waiting out the night here, like this—" Sebastian says. "It ain't an option."

Meza stands. Unholsters her Devastator. "Still got light. For now."

She marches down the aisle and toward the storage-bay-slash-workshop that takes up the back of the bus.

Sebastian darts after her, leaning against gravity to compensate for the awkward slant of the floor. He hastily slings his own Devastator, Captain, onto his back and checks Tennille, the Waster at his hip.

"And we do this fast," he says. "Like as-quick-as-the-ladies-fall-for-me fast."

"But without the subsequent disillusionment."

"Why are you so mean?"

HRM's storage bay is, as usual, at war with itself. Or rather, Sebastian and Meza's conflicting approaches to organizing a workspace are constantly bumping heads.

Sebastian has this crazy notion that tools and salvaged parts are significantly easier to find when one places them in their designated spaces. Meza defaults to, "I can find it so what's the problem?"

The windowless space is large but also cramped because… bus. Shelves and bins for the various salvage and scraps they've collected take up most of the space. Against a side wall extends a long workbench, one side tidy, the other a disaster.

Sebastian grabs a utility belt dripping with a few basic tools from a peg above his side of the workbench.

"Tell me we got a spare AFR," he says.

Replacing the regulator will be much faster than trying to fix it. And time is definitely a factor.

Meza plucks something from her sprawling chaos with sure hands. She holds up the airflow regulator, giving it a quick assessment.

Like most things in the Midlands, the small mechanical component looks like it has already lived a full, robust life and had expected to be retired and spending its twilight years surrounded by the grandkids by now. If there had ever been shine or luster to the vaguely L-shaped bit of tech, it would have been a long, long, *looong* time ago. But if Meza says it'll work, it'll work.

"It's the only spare we—what're you doing?" She eyes Sebastian as he secures the utility belt around his waist.

"Obviously I'm the one crawling under HRM."

Given their creepy surroundings, crawling into the dark shadows under the bus is riding high on his list of things he'd rather not do, but it is what it is.

"I can make the repair faster," she says.

"You're gonna make me say it, ain't you?"

"What?"

"You really think we have time for this?"

She cocks an eyebrow in question.

"Rour a memmer mor mah re," he mumbles.

"What?"

Sebastian rolls his eyes toward the ceiling. "You're a better shot than me. If anyone should have their blaster pointed at whatever might come jumping out at us from behind those rocks, it's obviously you. Ugh! Don't it get boring being a specimen of near perfection?"

"Not yet." She shoves the AFR into his hands and leads the way out the storage bay.

"Don't let it go to your head. You're only slightly better, and, at present, I'm way too freaked out by those giant rock thingies to be prideful."

They emerge through HRM's back door with Devastators

raised. Sebastian taps the door to secure the bus then pivots so that he and Meza are back-to-back. With blasters held shoulder-high and barrels following their lines of sight, they warily make their way around the bus's perimeter.

It's quiet. Eerie. Sebastian can't shake the feeling of being watched by more than the valley's silent, stony sentinels. He knows better than to tell himself that it's his imagination.

They make their way around the bus again. This go-round, Sebastian crouches to peer under HRM every few feet. Meza positions herself to stand over him each time, her eyes and blasters scanning their surroundings.

"We're clear," Sebastian says. Which is a good thing. Means he can crawl into the tight, shadowed space now. Hurray.

They agree that the best entry point is from the back.

The right side of the bus is at an angle that would require Sebastian to have the collapsible bones of a mouse to squeeze through. The driver's side is lifted off the ground quite nicely but leaves only a small wedge of space between the bus and the craggy cliff face.

Crawling under the bus from the back gives Sebastian space to get in there while also allowing Meza a good vantage point to keep an eye on their surroundings. All without completely cutting themselves off from HRM's entrance should they be descended upon by a horde of hellions—or whatever monsters this valley might decide to throw at them.

Sebastian has an uncomfortable thought. What would he do if Meza weren't here to watch his back right now? Which is a ridiculous question. He'd do the same thing as before she came around a few months ago. Get by.

"That's the only spare we got," Meza says. "Don't lose it. Don't break it."

"How incompetent do you think I am?"

Rather than answering, she narrows her eyes at him before turning to face the rock formations.

"I find your lack of faith disturbing."

Sebastian props Captain against the back of HRM. The large blaster will only make it harder for him to maneuver once he's under the bus. He grips Tennille. The Waster's size makes it better suited for small spaces.

He eyes the shadows beneath HRM.

He just needs to shimmy straight to the forward-left CGen, switch out the AFR faster than he's ever done anything in his entire life, and then shimmy right back out.

Helpfully, his brain pulls up every single messed-up story about people who've come to a nasty end because they crawled under their vehicle without realizing some small but horrifying creature was curled up beneath or crawling in the undercarriage.

Like the man who found himself stripped clean by a nest of bug-sized hellions who'd made a home in his vehicle's undercarriage. In five minutes, he was nothing but a pile of sticky bones.

Or the woman who realized her mistake and tried to scramble back to safety. Her friends tried frantically to pull the screaming woman out from under their vehicle. They half succeeded.

Sebastian grew up hearing stories of these nameless and unlucky victims of undercarriage monsters. Pretty effective cautionary tales, as far as he's concerned.

But not exactly the sort of thing he wants to be cataloging at this precise moment.

As he drops to the road and begins to crawl, he reminds himself that he's already checked under HRM, and nothing was there. And, anyway, they haven't been stopped five minutes. That can't be enough time for something to have gotten under there. Probably.

Shimmy. Switch. Back out.

Simple.

That's all he can allow himself to focus on.

Not on how even tiny monsters are deadly when they catch their victims off guard. Not on how that one type of hellion with long tentacles loves dragging victims into their waiting mouths.

And definitely not on how sludgebrains can bend and contort their bodies in utterly disturbing ways, making them impossibly agile.

Nope. He's definitely not thinking about any of that at all.

Between the fading light of day and the darkness of the valley, the shadows under HRM are solid. But Sebastian is certainly not sinking deeper into dread the farther he shimmies into the inky black.

No, sirree.

Shimmy. Switch. Back out. Simple.

The sunbaked road radiates heat from the day, but the warmth doesn't reach his bones. He activates his data cuff's holo-interface to chase away the nearest tendrils of shadow. It doesn't help his nerves as much as he would have liked.

"I'm surprised you done stuck around this long," Sebastian calls out.

"What?"

"I was thinking about what you said earlier. When you were all, 'What am I doing here?' If you're ready to go your own way, then it is what it is. But you know, when you first came aboard Her Royal Majesty, I always got the distinct impression you had one foot out the door."

She doesn't deny it.

He continues. "Figured you'd take off as soon as you found some town or caravan that'd have you. You stuck around for some reason. What you said got me to pondering as to what that reason might be."

As he moves closer to the front of the bus, the angle of the undercarriage tilts upward, giving him space to crawl in earnest.

"Fishing for a compliment?" Meza says. "Now?"

"So you got something nice to say about me?"

She says nothing for a moment. Sebastian imagines her grimace. It's nearly enough to chase away the heebie-jeebies.

Sebastian reaches the generator. He almost has enough space now to sit up straight. Almost. Placing Tennille on the ground next to him, he unfolds himself into an awkward hunched kneel in the tight space.

"That don't look too good," he mutters to himself. The CGen's vent shield is a mangled mess. They must have hit something. Maybe an especially aggressive boulder someone so rudely left out in the middle of the road.

With a few taps on his data cuff holo-interface, he pulls up HRM's schematics and sends the command for the CGen to open its vent shield, uncouple the AFR, and pop it out.

Nothing happens.

Stuck. Of course.

"Or maybe," he says, plucking a couple of tools from his belt and setting to work on prying open the remains of the vent shield, "you got so many nice things to say, you're overwhelmed and can't decide where to begin."

The soft crunching of gravel just beyond HRM betrays Meza's steady pacing. "I get that you like to chatter when you're nervous, but can you not right now?"

"Me? Nervous? No, ma'am. I am terrified. My goose bumps got goose bumps. My chills got chills. My tremors got tremors."

The vent shield falls to the cracked asphalt with a small clang. He probably won't be able to get it back on again. One more thing to be replaced. But not tonight.

He pulls the spare AFR from his utility belt before

reaching into the CGen to yank out the defective part. Even groping blindly, it should be easy to grab. It's nestled directly in the middle of the CGen.

Or at least…

It should be.

He feels around, not quite believing what his hand is telling him.

The old part isn't broken. It's missing completely.

"Okay," he says to himself. Unease stirs in his guts. "That's weird—"

A movement in the shadow.

Sebastian stills.

But only for a second before snatching up Tennille. He peers into the darkness, strains for the tiniest telltale sounds, reminds himself to breathe.

Nothing.

Whatever it is in the shadows with him, it's waiting too.

He swallows and stretches forward with the arm that wears the data cuff. The light of the holo-interface inches forward.

And illuminates the face of a grinning sludgebrain.

3

WHAT TO DO *When You Find Yourself in a Tight, Dark Spot with a Monster of Unspeakable Evil: A Guide Brought to You By a Guy Who Very Desperately Wants to Not Be in a Tight, Dark Spot with a Monster of Unspeakable Evil.* (Working title).

Step One: Freak all the way out.

Step Two: Okay, maybe not all the way out. Remember, at least, that you have a blaster pointed at it.

Step Three: Fire! Fire! Fire! *Pew pew! Pew pew pew!*

Step Four: Notice that your travel companion is on her stomach in the dirt with her Devastator, giving you cover and yelling for you to move your ass.

Step Five: Move. Your. Ass.

SEBASTIAN ROLLS OUT from under HRM and onto his feet, snatching Captain up from the road while he's at it. Swiftly holstering Tennille in a smooth, practiced motion, he points his Devastator at the opening beneath the bus.

Meza leaps to her feet. "Lost visual. Crawled out somewhere on the other side."

Shoulder to shoulder, they give the bus a wide berth. They wait with barrels pointed forward and fingers ready on their triggers. Everything is still.

It's the sort of quiet anticipation that precedes bad things. Lots of firing. Lots of fangs. Screaming. Snarling. Blood. Death. More screaming. Horror and horror with a side of horror. In other words, another day in the Midlands.

"Well, we're screwed," Sebastian offers.

"It's just the one."

"There's no way you can know that."

"I know," she says, so matter-of-factly Sebastian almost believes her.

"How exactly?"

"I just do."

"Convincing."

"If there were more, they'd already be on us."

"It ain't never just one sludgebrain." Sebastian puts his back to Meza's, Captain pointed toward the stone giants and that deep, deep blackness lurking between them.

The very last of the sky's warmth has given itself up to a dreary gray. And even that diffused glow has made up its mind to make itself scarce. HRM's head- and taillights flood this patch of the road with a harsh glare that darkens the shadows.

"I can't imagine what they're waiting for," he says, "but I strongly suggest we make a run for the back door while they're being coy."

"CGen fixed?"

"No, ma'am."

"Wanna trap ourselves inside a bus that ain't working and hope we can wait them out?"

"Option B," Sebastian says, "is to stand out here in the

open 'til they make their move and drag us off to a fate worse than death so—"

"Seba… stian… Yun…"

Sebastian swings Captain back around. The rasp had come from somewhere behind HRM.

The rasp that formed his name.

It's so unnerving that Sebastian has the urge to toss down his weapon, tell Meza, "Welp, I'm done," and lie down right there on the road to let whatever's about to happen next happen.

But this is one of their tricks. Of course it is.

Sludgebrains can't talk. Not really. They only mimic human speech. The sounds they make can fool the unwitting. They parrot the voice of a loved one crying for help. Call out in the sweet voice of a child. Wail like a baby just out of view.

People should know better by now, but there are still those who fling themselves into the trap. There's a technical term for those people. Idiots.

Have sludgebrains ever called a human by name?

Not that Sebastian has ever heard. Before today, that is.

"It… It musta heard you say my name earlier," he says.

Except, had Meza spoken his name at any point since they emerged from HRM?

"Ain't said your name," Meza says.

"And… Me… za…" The rasp reaches out from the darkness and runs an icy finger down Sebastian's spine.

"Welp," Sebastian says. "I'm done."

He does not, however, toss down his weapon and lie down right there on the road to let whatever's about to happen next happen.

"How about you, Meza? Seems like a mighty good time to mosey right back on inside, yeah?"

"No!" the creature calls. "Not leaving!"

A chill runs through Sebastian. This is not mimicry. The sludgebrain responded as if it understood.

"It… talks…" Sebastian says, stupidly.

"Yes. Talking. Stupid human is not hearing?"

"Okay. Rude."

The rudeness snaps Sebastian out of his stupor. Finally, something about this that makes sense. Sludgebrains never struck Sebastian as the kind and courteous types. That annoying habit they have of dragging humans off to a fate worse than death has done nothing for their reputation. So, of course, the first one he's ever talked to would be a jerk.

"You're alone, ain't you?" Meza says.

"Even if it is, why would it volunteer to let us know we outnumber it?"

"Out-number?" It makes a huffing, wheezing sound. A laugh? "We are alone."

"We?" Sebastian says. "Don't sound very alone to me. This thing is lying. And doing a really bad job of it."

"Not lying, stupid human." It has the nerve to sound offended. "Sebastian Yun is not understanding. We are saying alone because we are being alone."

"See! It did it again. How're you alone if you're talking in plural? By definition, plural means more than one. It ain't alone. It's lying. This is some kinda trap or mind game or… or… it's stalling! And we're playing right into it."

"Sebastian Yun is being stupid. Not understanding anything."

"Stop saying my name."

"Sebastian Yun."

"Stop it!"

"Sebastian Yun."

"Stop!"

"Sebastian Yun."

"I will kill you, you slimy puddle of goo— Oh my God. I

am arguing with a filthy sludgebrain. What is happening right now, Meza? Why am I arguing with a filthy sludgebrain?"

Meza's brow wrinkles. "Something's going on. Something… weird."

"Oh? You think so? Tell me more."

Ignoring his sarcasm, she takes a step toward HRM, and the sludgebrain hiding somewhere behind it.

Sebastian makes a sound of disapproval.

"Why do you know our names?" Meza asks.

"Sebastian Yun is saying it every day. Playing music. Saying names. Saying names. Playing music."

"You listen to Sebastian's show?"

"Listening always. Every day."

"You're a fan?" she says flatly. "Of that guy?"

"Why you gotta say it like that?" Sebastian mutters.

"Mmh… Fan." The creepy voice sounds thoughtful. "Yes. This is word."

"No." Sebastian shakes his head.

"What?" Meza asks him.

"I do not give that thing permission to be in my fan club."

"You even know what you're saying?"

"I do not. I don't know what I'm saying. I don't know what that thing is saying. I don't know why we're standing out here chatting it up instead of, I don't know—killing it dead, fixing Her Royal Majesty, and flying out of here as fast as we can."

"Sebastian Yun is not killing this Control," the creature says.

"Control?" Meza repeats.

"This Control is not killing Sebastian Yun and Meza. Being very cool, yes? Everyone being very cool."

"Right," Sebastian says. "Yes, of course. Everyone being very cool. The absolute coolest. But you have us at a disadvantage, Mr. Soulless Monster. How about you come out here real slow and introduce yourself to my good friends Captain and Tennille?"

"Quit messing around, Sebastian."

"I ain't never been more serious in my life."

"We don't wanna hurt you," Meza says to the hidden sludgebrain.

"I strongly disagree."

"Shut it."

Meza takes another step toward it. Sebastian presses his lips together. He doesn't like how the monster is drawing her in. Not at all.

"What's your name?" she asks.

"Don't go humoring it, Meza."

She cuts him a look that promises pain. Sebastian rolls his eyes but bites his tongue.

For a moment, the sludgebrain says nothing, but Meza waits. Until finally…

"Buddy."

Sebastian scoffs. "Buddy? You have got to be kidding me."

"Stupid human. Scott is calling me Buddy. We are liking."

"I like it too, Buddy," Meza says. "Who's Scott?"

"Will you stop asking it questions? That thing is obviously biding its time before more of its kind show up."

"Alone. We are saying and saying it. Stupid Sebastian Yun is not hearing."

"Let me handle this," Meza snaps. Then, in a much kinder voice—kinder than anything Sebastian ever knew she was capable of—she calls out to the creature, "How about we lower our weapons and you show yourself?"

And then she proceeds to lower her freakin' Devastator.

"Nope." Sebastian's grip tightens on his own blaster.

"Need a show of trust," she says. "On both sides."

"Do we though?"

"Why're you being difficult?"

"Well, I don't know. But I guess, if I had to put my finger on it, it's mostly because no one with a lick of sense and an ounce of survival instinct would trust a monster."

Meza turns to Sebastian, fully. Exposing her entire back to the unseen monster. Sebastian huffs a humorless laugh. She has picked a hell of a time to lose her mind. Timing really is everything.

"You trust me, don't you?" she says.

"Last I checked, you ain't a monster."

"You trust me because I make good calls."

"Yes. Until today, this very moment, when you decided to take a hard stand against common freakin' sense."

Meza glares, saying a million things without a single word. And one of those things is a warning.

They need to move things along. Step one. Take care of this sludgebrain problem.

"Fine," he says. "Let's try things your way."

She raises an eyebrow. Even Sebastian can admit he gave in way too easily.

"Really?"

Sebastian lowers his weapon.

"Really," he lies.

Meza turns back to HRM. "We won't hurt you. Both of us got our blasters lowered. Will you come out so we can see you?"

There's a pause, then the sludgebrain says, "Mmh. We are doing this."

The monster steps out from around HRM, passing through the glaring of the taillights.

Sebastian shouldn't be shocked at how young it looks. He knows these parasites are indiscriminate when it comes to plucking humans.

Still, to see the face of a kid that can't be a day over fifteen… It's wrong and gross and enraging.

Stringy blond hair falls past the sludgebrain's shoulders. It's tall and thin, like it doesn't get enough to eat. But looks are deceiving. Sludgebrains can transform their bodies in the blink of an eye. Even a skinny one like this has the potential to become something massive and overpowering.

It's covered in dirt and grime and what appears to be fresh blood. With satisfaction, Sebastian realizes that it's the monster's own blood. Its stolen flesh is covered with long tears and wide scrapes. It looked like something that's been dragged over a rocky road. But it carries itself completely upright as if it hasn't noticed its injuries.

Also, it's naked.

Totally and completely.

Because it's not enough to go around devouring and enslaving people. Sludgebrains have to make it weird for everyone involved by letting all their dangly bits hang loose.

The sludgebrain raises its hand in a stiff impersonation of a human greeting. "Hel—"

Sebastian raises his Devastator and fires. A lot.

The sludgebrain moves with eye-crossing speed.

It dodges most of the torrential blaster fire. A few lucky shots land but don't slow it down. Its hands and feet contort into grotesque shapes that allow it to easily half leap, half scale up the back of HRM.

"Sebastian!" Meza pushes Sebastian's weapon to the side.

He stops firing. Meanwhile, the sludgebrain vanishes over the bus's roof.

"Don't look at me like that, Meza! Daylight is officially gone. We gotta fix Her Royal Majesty and get out of here. And one less monster in the world ain't never a bad thing."

Her fist clenches at her side. But she doesn't raise it. He'll have to remember to thank her later for not slugging him. Her punches hurt.

"Ever hear of a sludgebrain talking to humans like this?" she says. "Neither have I."

"That don't change the fact that it's a sludgebrain."

"We gotta hear it out."

"Like hell! Allow me to remind you that sludgebrains only approach humans for one of two reasons. Because they're looking to add to their hive or because they're hungry."

"Yes." Buddy's rough voice carries over from the roof of the bus. "True. Sebastian Yun is saying true things. But…"

"But what exactly?" Sebastian says.

Its filthy face pops over the side, wearing a haughty expression. "We are letting Sebastian Yun and Meza be friends with us."

Sebastian fires. The messy blond mop disappears.

"Don't hurt it." Meza, once again, pushes his weapon to the side.

"We are liking Meza," the sludgebrain calls out. "Cooler than Sebastian Yun. Very."

"First of all," Sebastian says toward the roof. "Meza will never be cooler than Sebastian Yun." Then, to Meza, "More importantly, are you out of your mind?"

"No?" Buddy says.

"Not you. I already know you ain't out of anybody's mind, you evil parasite. That's sort of the problem." He turns his attention back to Meza. "Get it together. That ain't a person you're talking to. It's a big ol' glob of sentient snot that done oozed into some poor kid's brain and took over. We'd be doing that miserable puppet a favor by taking it out. And— And— What is it saying?"

Low muttering drifts down from HRM's roof. Sebastian can't make out the words, but it has the unmistakable cadence of two people going back and forth. But it's only the one voice, on both sides of the argument.

"Is it arguing?" Sebastian asks. "With itself?"

"You probably scared it."

"You do have a sense of humor after all."

Meza holsters her Devastator and raises both hands, as if to show the man-eating monster that she's no danger. "Can I come up there with you? Would that be okay? I'll leave my weapons down here. Just wanna talk."

Sebastian grabs her arm as if she might somehow leap up there in a single bound. "There is no way I'm letting you do that."

Meza's eyes travel slowly from his fist gripping her upper arm to his face. He chooses to ignore the inferred, "Wanna keep that hand?"

"Since when do I need your permission?" she asks.

"Since you obviously can't be trusted to not do something really dumb."

She snatches her arm back. "You're one to talk."

"Scott is not liking this. Sebastian Yun and Meza are stopping. No fighting."

"Who the hell is Scott?"

"Stop yelling at it!"

"Meza, two seconds ago, you weren't talking to me because of something idiotic I done pulled. Now you wanna sit down to tea with something like that? This your idea of getting back at me?"

"Believe it or not, everything ain't about you."

"Fine. But what went wrong in your brain to make you think you can trust a monster?"

She bristles. If her fury took physical form, it would be all prickly around her like a cactus.

"I'm-I-I-" She lets out an angry breath. "I don't know. I just do."

He shakes his head. "No way. That ain't good enough."

"Think I gotta explain myself to you?"

"If you—you, of all people! Smart, practical, killjoy Meza —wanna get yourself killed doing something stupid, I'm gonna have questions."

She crosses her arms, digs her heels into the spot. Immovable as a mountain. "You're so caught up in hating Buddy that you ain't paying attention to what's happening right now."

"I'm supposed to forget that it eats and enslaves people? People, by the way, is what we are. If it says grace before chow time, should we serve ourselves on a silver platter? Add a little garnish while we're at it?"

"Hunting humans sometimes, yes," Buddy says. "Good for eating. Good vessels. But we are never hunting you."

Meza gestures toward the sludgebrain as if it's making her case for her.

Sebastian throws up his hands as if to say it *so* isn't.

"Can't you see that this one is different?" she asks.

"I'm sure it's a very special snowflake and all that, but it's still a freakin' monster. Ergo, it is evil. Ergo, we kill it. Ergo, unless you want to die. Ergo, I don't think you do."

"Using that word wrong."

"You get my point."

"Clearly not all monsters want to be monsters," she says.

"Are you listening to yourself?"

"Every time some whim of yours leads to trouble, I'm there with you. You won't even consider my crazy idea."

"'Cuz there's such a thing as too crazy," Sebastian says. "Standing in the middle of nowhere after sunset arguing for monster rights lands squarely under too crazy. I mean, c'mon, Meza, couldn't you wait until after you abandon me to completely lose it?"

"Abandon you?"

Sebastian rolls his eyes. "I was being hyperbolic. Obviously."

"We are trusting Meza."

Sebastian jumps back at the unexpected proximity of the sludgebrain, which is suddenly standing right behind Meza. He lifts his weapon.

Meza has the nerve to look pleased—without smiling, of course.

The sludgebrain, however, is smiling. Not a giant smile. It's a small, close-lipped thing. Almost fragile.

Head lowered, shoulders hunched, its eyes flit up to steal glances at Sebastian and Meza before finding the ground again. It's as if the sludgebrain has transformed into a younger, more nervous version of itself.

"We are deciding to coming down," it says. "With Meza."

"Meza," Sebastian says. "Step this way. Now."

She moves, but only to block Sebastian's shot even more. He lets out a growl of frustration.

"Glad you decided to come down," she says. "Never met anything—anybody—like you. You really listen to Sebastian's show?"

It nods. "Hello, fellow post-apoca-lyptizens."

Its eyes flicker up before lowering again. A flash of ragged, sharklike teeth shatter any illusion of boyishness in its shy grin.

"How?" Meza asks. "Sludgebrains use human tech?"

"Not needing." It taps its ear. "We are hearing. Humans very noisy. Talking on human tech always."

"You mean like radio signals," Meza says. "Electromagnetic waves. You all naturally pick up on walkie-talkie communication. That sort of thing."

It bobs its head in confirmation. "Very annoying. And very boring. Not *So You Survive End of World*. Different. We are liking. Listening always. From very beginning."

"That's why you're talking to us?"

Another nod.

Meza opens her mouth to say something, closes it again. Sebastian is used to her silence, but this is the first time he's seen her speechless. It occurs to him that she's... excited? Maybe even happy? Though no one would know it to look at her.

Could he have it wrong? Is Meza right about this sludgebrain?

No, that's ridiculous. Utterly so. The most ridiculous thought to ever cross his mind.

"I got a question too," Sebastian says, though he looks pointedly at Meza when he asks. "How long before you drop the farce and infest us?"

"Infesting? We are not doing. Never doing alone. Not bonding. Not eating. Very bad. Unless we are having emergency. We are bringing humans home. To Harmony. Voice is deciding what is happening to humans. Always. We are not Voice. Only Hunter."

"Is that supposed to make me feel better?" Sebastian asks.

Buddy's eyebrows crinkle together, confused. "We are answering question."

"Got a lot I want to ask you," Meza says, retaking control of the conversation. "But Sebastian's right. About one thing at least. Ain't safe for us to be out here like this. We gotta fix the bus."

"Finally," Sebastian says. "She sees reason."

Buddy goes very still. It cocks its head to the side as if listening to something.

Sebastian narrows his eyes at it. "What's up with the creature of unspeakable evil?"

"It ain't evil." But Meza is watching the sludgebrain closely now too.

The sludgebrain's entire demeanor changes. Gone is the

sheepish version of itself. Its back straightens, and it takes on an air of self-importance that matches Sebastian's first impression of it.

"Sebastian Yun and Meza are going. Now." It thrusts a hand forward and opens its palm, revealing an AFR identical to the one missing from the forward-left CGen. "You are having this back."

Meza snatches it up. "This ain't the spare. And it's wrecked."

"How'd you get this?" Sebastian asks.

"We are hearing Sebastian Yun talking. For show. Knowing we are close. Scott is wanting to meet—"

"Who the hell is Scott?"

"You are meeting already, stupid human. Not paying attention."

Sebastian's brain catches up with something else the sludgebrain said. "Wanting to meet— You caused our crash!"

"Yes. We are jumping on Her Royal Majesty. Crawling under. Hurting our body. Very much. Then we are taking something. Meza is having it now."

The sludgebrain grabs Meza's hand, the one holding the AFR, and closes its dirty, bloody fist over hers.

"Hey!" Sebastian whips his Devastator toward Buddy. "No touchy!"

But as Buddy stares down at Meza, something passes between them. Her eyes widen. Understanding.

"Meza is fixing. Go now. Yes."

"More sludgebrains are coming," Meza says. "They're coming now."

Buddy nods.

"You ain't gonna tell us they're 'friendly' like you?" Sebastian asks.

Buddy hesitates. "Hunters. Not friendly."

"Where's the spare?" Meza asks Sebastian.

Sebastian reaches into the utility belt pouch where he'd stuffed the AFR. It's empty. He pats frantically at all the pockets. He looks toward HRM, to the span of darkness underneath. He must have dropped it during the scramble to get away from their unexpected guest.

Meza is already dashing toward the bus. "Don't shoot Buddy, Sebastian. It's gonna help you watch the perimeter."

"Since when did we become a team?"

"Since you agreed not to shoot it." She scrambles under the bus, disappearing from view entirely.

"I did not agree to that!" Sebastian calls after her, then re-centers his blaster on the sludgebrain and repeats, "I did not agree to that."

Buddy doesn't react to the weapon pointed at it. It stares at the shadowy rock formations. If sludgebrains were capable of emotion, Sebastian would describe the expression on its face as dread.

But what does a sludgebrain dread? Clothes? Soap and water?

It doesn't make sense. It'll be Buddy's own friends making an appearance. Why isn't it happy for the reunion?

Buddy's eyes fall to the darkness beneath HRM, defeated. "No time."

And that's when Sebastian feels it.

For humans, there's plenty in this world worth dreading. Only one sensation in itself is feared and also inspires fear.

It's a nonsound. Something like a ringing in the ear but not like that at all. A nonfeeling that's a little like light-headedness but absolutely nothing like it. Sometimes, it starts off so faint, a person could fail to notice it altogether.

But ignoring it is never an option. Because this nonheard/nonfelt... *thing,* this *Dissonance* doesn't always precede an attack, but it only ever happens when a pack of sludgebrains is near.

With the Dissonance filling his head, Sebastian turns to the sludgebrain. "So much for you being alone."

"Sebastian Yun is trusting this Control, yes?" For some reason, Buddy is whispering.

Sebastian takes careful steps away from Buddy and backs toward HRM, where Meza had crawled under the bus. He doesn't take Captain off the sludgebrain.

"I knew this was a trap," he says. "Though my imminent demise does take all the fun right out of this told you so."

"Not trapping, stupid human." Still whispering, its words come out faster. More urgent. "We are helping Sebastian Yun and Meza. Having plan. First, Sebastian Yun is dropping weapon."

"Ha!"

"Sebastian Yun is trusting us. Please."

"The only monster I trust is a dead one."

And now, he decides, is an opportune time to build that trust.

Sebastian pulls the trigger.

4

BUDDY SEEMS to move even before Sebastian's finger has fully squeezed the trigger. The blaster fire hits nothing. Captain flies from Sebastian's hands.

He reaches for Tennille, but Buddy is too fast. It snatches the Waster away without Sebastian getting off a single shot.

"I knew you couldn't be trusted, you—"

A monstrous hand whips out and wraps around Sebastian's throat, lifts him up. Sebastian's feet scrabble for ground, his boots barely scraping against the cracked, uneven pavement. He scratches and beats against Buddy's hands. The effort is wasted.

Buddy snarls, the mask of civility gone. Trap sprung.

With a pair of heavy thuds, two new sludgebrains make their presence known. They crouch on HRM's roof, shrouded in shadow and glowering down on the scene below them. Their lips move, almost as if they're whistling, but no sound comes out.

Buddy purses its lips to nonwhistle back, then points to the darkness beneath HRM.

The glare Sebastian gives Buddy would surely make Meza

proud. His voice is a gasping wheeze. "You... really... are... the worst."

With another snarl, Buddy drops Sebastian.

He lands hard, gasps for air, and takes in a lungful of dust from the sand-covered road. His coughing fit squeezes water from his eyes. With unsteady arms, he attempts to pick himself up. Buddy's foot comes down on his back, pinning him flat.

One of the new sludgebrains jumps from HRM. This one has infested a middle-aged woman with unkempt brown hair. Or at least, Sebastian thinks it's the form of a middle-aged woman.

The body has been transformed. Its muscles are stretched and bulging to such an exaggerated degree that one prick from a pin might pop them. Its legs bend the wrong way, shaped more like a dog or cat's than anything remotely human, and its arms are so long its knuckles almost drag along the road.

Its face remains unsettlingly human, the softness of the woman's round face at odds with the twisted sharpness of its body. It crouches down and creeps toward HRM. Toward Meza.

"Hey, Sasquatch!" Sebastian shouts at it, voice rough from breathing in too much dust. "I think the Hendersons are looking for you. You hit every branch falling out the ugly tree or what? Ever consider signing up for a beauty pageant? Don't ignore me!"

It ignores him.

"I know you understand me! You— Oof!" Buddy's foot comes down on Sebastian, cutting him off. Not that Sebastian's attempts to draw the middle-aged-looking sludgebrain's attention has been doing much.

He'd been picturing a scenario where Meza remains hidden long enough to surprise their guests with some crazy road warrior goddess move that gets them out of this still alive. And, more importantly, still human.

Of course Buddy had to go and dash that hope. The last of that pipe dream deflates as the middle-aged one flattens itself and crawls under HRM.

The shadows beneath the bus light up with pinging blaster fire. The sludgebrain springs out from under HRM, hissing and scowling.

From the roof, the second sludgebrain makes that creepy huffing sound that Sebastian interprets as laughter. It grins widely, nearly doubled over. Long, unruly red hair shakes with its bobbing head.

The middle-aged one snaps a silent whistle toward the redhead.

Still laughing, the redhead straightens. This monster wears a pale, freckle-smattered female body that's been stretched like Elastigirl. Legs, limbs, torso, even its neck all elongated, it's no less than seven feet tall.

Instead of bulking out like the middle-aged one, its muscles are pulled taut. Still, the definition is so exaggerated, Sebastian could count the sinews even from this distance.

This whole overly defined muscle look is a favorite among their kind. It's like they all read the same late twentieth-century shonen manga and decided, "Hey, yeah. That's where it's at!"

The redhead strides to the other side of HRM's roof, shrinking down as it moves. It nods at the middle-aged one then leaps down the other side.

A few seconds later, there's a snarl and then more flashing blaster fire.

The middle-aged one crouches back down to crawl under HRM.

"Mez— Ooof!"

Buddy's foot comes down hard on Sebastian again, effectively cutting off his warning. Then it's too late.

The middle-aged one scurries back out into the open, dragging Meza by a leg. Meza's hands are empty as she's hauled backward, but she struggles and kicks at the sludgebrain.

It drops her foot, looking more annoyed than harmed by her fighting.

Meza pivots on the ground and pulls out her Devastator.

The redheaded sludgebrain drops down behind her. Rips the weapon away. The shot goes wide.

The middle-aged one snatches Meza up and yanks her out of sight. Sebastian doesn't have to wonder for long where it's taking her. Buddy plucks him up and drags him in the same direction. They're both unceremoniously deposited on the side of the road. Farther away from HRM. Away from their weapons.

They land in an ungainly sprawl. Sebastian's face finds a soft landing on her stomach, at least. A welcome change from his cheek being smashed into the road's rough gravel. Though his derrière in the air doesn't leave him much dignity to salvage.

"Hey," Sebastian says.

"Hey," Meza answers.

Straightening herself into a sitting position, she gives Sebastian little choice but to right himself as well.

Meza levels an even stare at the middle-aged one. Her face doesn't betray so much as a tick of apprehension or anger. She's preternaturally calm. And of course she is. This is Meza, after all.

The middle-aged one starts to turn away but gives Meza a second, perplexed glance. Unsettled, perhaps? Maybe this is its first time coming across a human so seemingly unaffected by her own impending doom.

Sebastian knows from experience that Meza's unreal calm in situations like this can take some getting used to.

Whatever's going through the middle-aged one's mind, it seems to shake off its thoughts before looking over both their heads.

That's when Sebastian notices a fourth sludgebrain creeping up behind them.

It's completely nude, of course. Just like all the others.

So.

Much.

Nudity.

This one wears a dark-skinned male's form, its black hair cropped short in messy, coarse tufts. Its muscles are so ballooned that even the most gung ho Old World body-builder would see it and say, "Wow, dude. There's such a thing as too far." Sebastian wonders how it even walks.

Its paradoxical agility shows even in the small motions of hunching down and stalking forward. It doesn't stop until it's within arm's reach. Even hunched over, it looms above the sitting Sebastian and Meza.

A growl rumbles from its throat, low and sinister. It gives them each a long, hard glare. The threat is clear.

Sebastian reaches the conclusion that it would behoove him to remain very, very still and say nothing. Let there be no mistake that he understands its implicit instructions.

Don't move. Don't try anything.

He calls to mind everything he knows about how sludge-brains work. Which, admittedly, is not a lot. It isn't as though tons of humans get the chance to stroll through a sludge-brain hive and come back to spill the deets.

One thing he knows is that he and Meza still have time. Sludgebrains neither devour nor infest humans where they find them. A fact that Buddy confirmed moments ago.

Nope, their MO is to drag humans away. Presumably to one of their underground hives.

Not to say there are never corpses left behind after a sludgebrain attack. Those corpses are always clutching their weapons. These creatures prefer to herd their humans, but that doesn't mean they're against outright killing humans who aren't worth the trouble of keeping alive.

Sebastian has no idea where the nearest hive is or how long it'll take to get there, but he and Meza aren't dead yet. And they get to remain human for a little while longer. There's a way out of this. They'll be good, until the right opportunity presents itself.

The moment the big, bulky guy takes its eyes off them, it seems to dismiss Sebastian and Meza's presence entirely. It straightens, steps over them, and then it's Buddy's turn to be on the receiving end of that thing's attention.

Buddy shrinks down as the big, bulky guy towers over it and "whistles" something. Buddy responds and the big guy's demeanor changes.

With a huffing laugh, it throws a gigantic arm around Buddy's neck and pulls it into a hold that would crush its throat, were Buddy human.

The redhead, grinning, leaps onto Buddy's back. Then the middle-aged one jumps in. Soon, it's a melee. Teeth snap, claws swipe. They pounce and tumble. But through it all, they're laughing and smiling.

It's… playful?

Sebastian shakes his head.

No. That's a word for describing frolicking puppies and kittens. Not a pack of soulless monsters.

This is far from what Sebastian expected, but if they're in no hurry to haul him and Meza off to their hive, who is Sebastian to look this gift horse in the mouth?

Plus, if they'll be busy doing… whatever this is for a

while, that gives Sebastian and Meza a few minutes to confer.

Eying the wrestling sludgebrains, Sebastian scoots a tiny bit closer to Meza.

None of the monsters so much as twitch a brow in their direction. Sebastian scoots again, then again. With still no reaction from their captors, he scoots the rest of the way until there's no space left to scoot.

"For the record," Sebastian whispers, "I gave very specific instructions not to set the data rings off before dawn."

"What?" Meza says.

"When I slipped Manny those data rings. Back at the Anti-Techer town." Or, at least, Sebastian's pretty sure he had. "Whatever. Manny shoulda known better."

"Manny?"

"That jerk face of a town leader's son. Can you imagine having that woman for a mother? The poor kid was so miserable. I saw that immediately when she came out with her posse to shove their superiority in our faces."

Meza gives him a long look before turning back to watch the scuffling sludgebrains. "Wanna know how much I care about that right now?"

"Since we're definitely about to die, or worse, I thought I'd be nice and offer you a chance to acknowledge that I ain't completely responsible for this evening's turn of events."

"Because clearing your name is our highest priority."

"I'm just saying, Manny didn't follow instructions."

Manny clearly kept to the first half of Sebastian's plan. Take the handful of data rings Sebastian provided and discreetly tuck them in the various nooks and crannies around the town. Then, if things had gone according to plan, in the *morning*—i.e. not a mere two hours after he'd received them—Manny would have hit Play on the preloaded playlist, which would have blasted through the synced data rings.

That whole being-chased-by-a-mob thing would have happened by the light of day instead of during the settling of twilight. Some people are so inconsiderate.

Sebastian absently rubs at his temples. He's never felt the Dissonance this long. The sensation doesn't hurt, but it's annoying.

"So all of this is Manny's fault." Meza's tone is flat, turning the question into a statement.

"Oh, good. You agree. I'm glad that in our last hour, we can get on the same page about this."

He almost says more. About the other thing that pushed him to his brilliant but *possibly* shortsighted actions. It was what the town leader said about him, how she said it. But that would almost be like him saying he believed her words. And he didn't.

He eyes the blasters abandoned on the road. Captain, Tennille, and Meza's blasters are in a careless pile near HRM. All he'd have to do is inch past the sludgebrain melee, and those weapons are his. So, yeah. Definitely won't be getting his hands on those anytime soon.

Sebastian wonders which way the sludgebrains will take him and Meza when they're ready to move out. He hadn't seen where they'd come from. They might as well have dropped from the night sky.

Except for that big, bulky one. It had come from behind where he and Meza are sitting.

He glances into the darkness over his shoulder.

"Whoa!" His heart leaps into his throat.

A new sludgebrain crouches mere feet away from him. This one is in a slim, female body. It maintains a mostly human appearance with a long curtain of black hair covering all but a sliver of its face. The dark strands pool on the ground around its dirt-stained hands and feet.

Sebastian is reminded of a character he saw in a movie

that got under his skin so badly he nearly swore off all Old World videos.

And it's just *watching* him.

"How long has that been there?"

"A while," Meza says.

"And you couldn't say something about it?"

She shrugs. "What would you've done about it?"

"Shoo!" Sebastian swats a hand toward it. Without getting too close, of course. "Scat! Go play!"

This sludgebrain—Ringu, Sebastian thinks to call it, and once the idea strikes him, he can't *not* call it that—tilts its head. Its sheets of tangled black hair shift with the movement.

Ringu jolts closer. Sebastian startles away from it, into Meza. She doesn't budge.

"Stay calm," she says.

"I really don't wanna," he whispers.

But he reminds himself that sludgebrains don't eat or infest people where they find them and holds his breath as the sludgebrain leans in way too close. Unblinking, it studies Sebastian.

Ringu reaches up with a grimy hand. It's all Sebastian can do to not puke as it runs a finger down his cheek. It pokes at Sebastian's middle, picks up strands of Sebastian's dark, slightly too-long hair. Lets them drop. It tugs at his clothes, then presses in so close that its unkempt strands brush over Sebastian. Their noses almost touch.

A grin shows through its disheveled waves of dark hair. Sebastian isn't sure if it really has that many sharp and ragged teeth or if he's seeing double.

"He...llo..." Its words are halting and awkward. "Se...ba... stian... Yun."

Sebastian crumples away from its rank, hot breath. "Oh,

thank God. I'll die of asphyxiation before y'all turn me into a meat suit."

Everything is suddenly quiet. The sludgebrains are no longer tussling.

Three sets of monster eyes that had previously not given him a second glance now fall on Sebastian.

"Se...ba...stian... Yun..." one mimics. Then the others join in, feeling out and growing slightly more comfortable with the syllables of his name as they repeat it. "Se...ba...stian... Yun... Se-ba...stian... Yun... Se-ba-stian... Yun... Se-ba-stian... Yun."

The fourth set of eyes, belonging to the sludgebrain at the bottom of the dogpile, zeros in on the ground with suspicious focus.

"Don't tell me," Sebastian says. "More fans."

Or maybe not.

Those three sets of eyes drop away from him to fall on that sludgebrain at the bottom of the dogpile.

Their playfulness is gone. As they disentangle, Buddy raises its hands, placating. The other sludgebrains lob a barrage of silent whistles at it.

The redhead—Carrie, Sebastian decides to call it—is the only one grinning. It looks from Sebastian to Buddy as if in on some joke. Whatever it's saying seems less heated than the other two.

The middle-aged one, which Sebastian dubs Misery, seems to have gotten itself all worked up. Its lips contort quickly as it whistles, its gestures big and expressive.

The big, bulky guy—Children of the Corn, because... well, Sebastian likes a theme, and it's the next horror movie title that pops to mind, and, look, he has things other than naming random sludgebrains to think about right now.

Children of the Corn snaps at Misery. But when it turns

back to Buddy and whistles something, it embodies calm even though its brows are furrowed in question.

"This Control... fan..."

Sebastian startles. Not that he'd forgotten Ringu at his side. It's simply a sign of how creepy this particular sludgebrain is. Sebastian can't help but flinch at every movement, every word from this thing.

"Last... hunting time..." Ringu says. "Hunter Find... sharing... *So You Survive... End of World*. Sharing... human... music. Sharing... Se-ba-stian... Yun... We are... listening... This Control... listen-ing most... of all. Fan... most... of... all."

"Right," Sebastian says, brain struggling through Olympian-level contortions to follow the sludgebrain's strange way of speaking. He glances at Meza, but her stoic expression reveals nothing of what she thinks about this sludgebrain or its offering of information.

"Look, Ringu—"

"Rin...gu?"

"Don't worry about it." Most humans don't get Sebastian's myriad of Old World references. No way he expects a sludgebrain to get it. "Since you're a fan, you mind filling me in on what's going on over there?"

He nods toward the bickering—at least he's pretty sure they're bickering—monsters.

Ringu grins through its curtain of black hair. It doesn't look away from Sebastian.

"Asking... why... Hunter Find... not tell-ing... this human is Se-ba-stian... Yun... Weird... Very..."

Sebastian looks from Ringu to the other sludgebrains and back to Ringu. As near as he can figure, Hunter Find must be what they call Buddy.

"Why's that weird?" he asks.

"First Hunter Find.... is talking... to humans..." Ringu

points to Sebastian. "Weird… Yes… Hunter Find… saying… new trick. Good trick… for… trap-ping humans… Hunter Shriek is… believing… Until now."

Sebastian glances at the huddle of sludgebrains again. Hunter Shriek must be the big, bulky one who seems to be in charge. Aka Children of the Corn.

"Hunter Find… strange… Listen-ing… to… human show… weird. Sharing human… show… weird. Talk-ing to… humans… weird. Doing all… weird, weird, weird… Very bad… Maybe… Hunter Shriek… deciding."

Sebastian pieces together the disjointed flow of information as best he can.

Hunter Find, aka Buddy, told the rest of its Hunter friends that it was trying out a new trick on the humans. They bought it. Until Ringu revealed that one of the humans they captured is none other than Sebastian Yun, radio host extraordinaire.

Which is only significant because after telling the sludge-brains to give *So You Survived the End of the World* a listen, they know Buddy is basically obsessed with Sebastian, a human.

Chatting it up with a human may have been odd behavior to start with. Putting this together with the rest of it apparently doesn't add up to a good look for Buddy.

"You ain't worried about what they'll think about you, my self-professed biggest fan, talking to me?"

Ringu blinks as if the thought hadn't occurred to it. Maybe this one isn't the sharpest rock in the desert. And maybe Sebastian should've kept that thought to himself. Unnerving it may be, but this sludgebrain is making itself useful.

Ringu's face darkens. Perhaps thinking through the repercussions of its actions.

Meza elbows Sebastian. As if he needs his verbal blunder pointed out to him.

"Hey, don't worry," Sebastian says to Ringu. "They're so busy with Bud—Hunter Find. You're totally fine. Trust me." He puts on his most charming smile.

Ringu only stares.

Sebastian can't trust Ringu any more than he does Buddy, but maybe he can use it.

He glances at the other sludgebrains, double-checking that they remain completely engrossed in their Buddy problem, then lowers his voice.

"You really like *So You Survived the End of the World*, right?"

Ringu nods.

"You like all the music?"

Another nod.

"And, of course, you like me. I am the show."

A third nod.

"You realize, if anything happens to me, that's it. The fun is over. No more Sebastian Yun for you. You don't want that, do you?"

A head shake this time, eyes gaping.

Sebastian lowers his voice even more. "Then how about we do something to make sure that don't happen?"

Ringu stares. Sebastian isn't sure this means it's down for a little rebellion, is considering the proposal, or thinks that Sebastian has lost his mind. But he and Meza have nothing to lose at this point. He presses on.

"All I need is a little distraction. We can be subtle, you know. It don't have to look like you're in cahoots with me."

There's an especially loud snarl. Sebastian jumps, turning back to the other sludgebrains. Misery charges at Buddy. The only thing that stops the attack is Carrie snaking out a hand to stop it. Someone has a temper.

"What're they saying now?" Sebastian asks.

"Hunter Find... saying and saying... Se-ba-stian... Yun not... ma-ttering. Just... stupid hollow... Hunter Strong angry... saying... Hunter Find... problem... Saying Hunter Shriek... soft. Wanting... to kill Se-ba-stian... Yun... Teaching... Hunter Find lesson."

"I do not like the sound of that."

Based on body language, Sebastian guesses that Hunter Strong is the one he's been calling Misery.

"Hunter Find... saying... killing human waste-ful. Saying... Hunter Strong... stupid... Bad at job."

"That definitely sounds like Buddy."

Suddenly, Misery's muscles balloon and bulge. It grows a foot, maybe two, and shoves Carrie away. Slamming Buddy to the ground, it opens its mouth wide and seems to shout.

Or maybe it's a roar.

Hard to say since, like their whistled language, Sebastian hears nothing. But the steady feel of the Dissonance spikes, increasing the uncomfortable pressure in his skull.

Ringu winces, a hand going to its head. Carrie has a similar reaction. Buddy, receiving the brunt of whatever this is, grimaces and thrashes. Its figure bulks up, and it pushes at Misery. The attempt to topple the angry sludgebrain is weak. Misery doesn't let up.

"What is happening?" Sebastian looks to Meza with wide eyes.

She shakes her head, clearly as baffled as Sebastian.

Children of the Corn, the only sludgebrain unaffected, marches over to Misery and pulls it off Buddy, gives it a good shake. Misery's mouth snaps shut. The Dissonance in Sebastian's head levels out.

"What was that?" Sebastian asks.

Ringu's eyes take a moment to refocus, then its mouth spreads into its ragged grin. "Di-strac-tion."

It lunges. Sebastian's arms spring up to defend himself,

but Ringu knocks him aside. Sebastian has barely registered that he isn't under attack when Meza's solid warmth is replaced with empty air.

Suddenly, she's near HRM, where the weapons have been dropped haphazardly. Ringu pushes a blaster into Meza's hands.

Just as abruptly, Ringu is back at Sebastian's side.

It whistles at the others, catching their attention. Then points at Meza.

Meza quickly recovers from this unexpected turn. She aims Captain at the surprised sludgebrains. They scatter as she fires.

Leaving Buddy behind, the three other sludgebrains split off. Two draw Meza's fire, while the third circles behind her.

"No!" Sebastian races toward Meza.

Something collides into him, and his whole world turns topsy-turvy. He catches a final, jarred glimpse of Meza with three sludgebrains converging on her. Then, he's swallowed by shadows.

5

THE DARKNESS IS SO COMPLETE, Sebastian can't see so much as an outline of his own hands. There's no separation between himself and the dark. He might have to start doubting his existence.

Though the lingering sting of his less-than-gentle landing against something hard and rough staves off any impending existential crisis. Nothing says "Yep, you're real" like pain does.

After the stomach-twisting whir of motion and the feeling of flying, this stillness is an unsettling companion to the darkness.

He'd been carried off by a sludgebrain. That much his mind managed to put together when he realized those big shadows whizzing by were the rock formations he'd seen from the bridge. But then those were gone and only deep, impenetrable black surrounded him as the sludgebrain whisked him farther and farther away.

Sebastian tries to guess how far he was carried, or for how long. It's impossible to tell. The ride seemed to both end as soon as it started and stretch on for a heart-stopping eternity.

Now, he's wherever this is. And the sludgebrain is…

He doesn't like the open-ended nature of that little detail.

With a flick of his wrist, his holo-interface bursts to life with a blinding glow. He squeezes his eyes shut and snaps his head away from the sudden contrast. The back of his head makes sharp contact with something hard and unforgiving. Lightning cracks across his skull.

Sebastian lets out a string of curses to retaliate against the reality-affirming pain. Then a few more to protest against this whole stupid, freakin' situation.

Blink, blink, blinking until the spot in his vision clears, he slowly makes out forms etching themselves into being around him.

There's a pillar of rock protruding from the ground. Another pillar of rock protruding from the ground. Oh, and what surprise, another pillar—

No, wait.

That's a—

He yelps and jerks back. The same spot on the back of his head hits against the same hateful chunk of rock. That rock, he's now convinced, definitely has it out for him.

Ringu squats not an arm's length away. Staring at him. As still and expressionless as the stalagmites around them. Sebastian freezes.

The glow of his holo-interface, though practically a mini sun in this darkness, is hardly a floodlight. It casts its illumination a few yards in all directions, giving every stony column and jaggy crag it touches long black shadows. Then the blue light tapers off, giving way to a nightmarish unknown.

With neither stars nor moon above, it's clear that Ringu has brought him somewhere underground. Which isn't a total shocker. Underground is where sludgebrains hang out and where they were first unearthed.

Story goes that sludgebrains were the third and final nail in civilization's brimming coffin.

After the AI the world depended on went all murderous and after some folks too smart for their own good poked monster-spewing holes in the fabric of reality, another really smart group of people came along with another brilliant idea.

These geniuses thought maybe underground was the place to be. Back then, folks still had the technology to burrow deep, deep underground and, potentially, make a new life there. Let the flatliners and hellions have whatever—and whoever—is left topside. Not their problem.

Because, as it would turn out, these subterranean trailblazers had the honor of unleashing a brand-new problem upon the survivors of the first and second apocalypses.

Deep, deep, *deep* under Earth's crust waited colonies of living goop with a remarkable ability to cling to life for millennia on top of millennia in a dormant state.

And thus the world received a resounding answer to an age-old question. Yes, everything and anything could always get much, much worse.

Sebastian has a sneaking suspicion that he won't be a fan of whatever reason Ringu has for bringing him down here. Honestly, there can only be so many explanations for why a sludgebrain would go out of its way for alone time with a human.

For now, the sludgebrain is back to staring at Sebastian with unblinking devotion.

Sebastian lets out a shaky breath. Borrows some of that unnatural calm Meza musters in times like this. Meza… left on her own to face a whole pack of those monsters. Thanks to this monster.

"This wasn't in the plan I had in mind, douchenoggin."

Ringu continues to stare.

"I'd love to believe you whisked me away due to an overwhelming concern for and commitment to my well-being, but I ain't never been much of an optimist."

He reaches behind his head and rubs the sore spot on the back of his skull. Ringu mimics the gesture. Sebastian's hand stills. Ringu follows suit. When Sebastian tilts his head, Ringu does the same, like a repulsive reflection.

"Congratulations. You are the architect of the creepiest moment of my life. Quite the feat, considering the things I done survived."

The sludgebrain, naturally, offers no response.

"I ain't scared of you. You think sludgebrains are the biggest, baddest things out there? Not by a long shot. There's a monster I reckon even the likes of you don't wanna tangle with. I lived through a run-in with one of them bastards when I was still a little ol' thing. So pardon me if I waive the option to quake in my boots just 'cuz you wanna play a game of monster see, monster do."

"M… mm… mmmine…" Ringu says.

Don't ask. Don't ask. Don't ask.

"What?" Sebastian asks.

It grins. The harsh blue light distorts shadows between its messy rows of ragged-sharp teeth.

"Seb-ast-ian… Yun… M-mine."

"Alrighty. You done called my bluff. I'm, like, two seconds away from pissing my pants."

It shifts forward, dropping to all fours as it stalks toward Sebastian. It inches forward on its fingers and toes as if to specifically remind Sebastian of how not human it is.

Reminder. Not. Needed.

Thanks.

And that dead-eyed stare? Not any more fun in a dark cave than it had been on a desolate road.

It creeps closer, closer, closer until its nose presses directly against Sebastian's neck. It takes a long, indulgent sniff. The unruly black hair prickles Sebastian's chin.

He adds this to his list of not-fun things.

But he doesn't dare move, fully aware that this thing's nasty teeth are directly below that nose.

"Didn't even buy me a drink fir—"

He clamps down on his muttered words as the sludge-brain's wide tongue unfurls and mops a warm, sticky trail around his throat, over his jawline, and up the side of his face.

Sebastian swallows. "Honest fellow that I am, I feel a moral obligation to inform you that I taste terrible. It's all the bitterness I been stewing in practically my whole life. Nothing but heartache in my tragic backstory. Makes a guy real gamy. And I doubt I got any nutritional value on account of how I never eat my veggies. Don't you think you deserve better? I think you deserve better."

"Not... eating."

"When you say I'm yours, you can't mean— Look, I'm flattered. I get it. I'm utterly irresistible. And you know, if we were the same species, maybe. But as it is, you just ain't my type. I prefer ladies who ain't got the stench of human flesh on their breath. No offense."

Ringu pulls back, but it's still uncomfortably close when it says, "We are... being... Se-ba-stian... Yun."

There it is. The fate worse than death. Anything would be better than being infested by a sludge. *Anything.*

It's an existence so vile, Sebastian refuses to let his mind go there. Not now. Not if he doesn't want to collapse into a ball of despair and self-pity. Which wouldn't be the most useful thing just now.

He continues to play dumb.

"Oh, is that all? Why didn't you just say so, friend? I'm more than happy to take you on as a mentee, teach you to live life to your fullest Sebastian Yun potential. Matter of fact, I been contemplating penning a book on the subject.

"Reckon I'll call it something like *Sebastian Yun's Guide to Living Your Best Life in the New Dark Age*. Working on the title. Hey, I'll mention you in the dedication. 'For Ringu. You are the wind beneath my wings.' You'd like that, wouldn't you?"

"Bonding with… Se-ba-stian… Yun." It taps its head, then reaches out and presses the same fingertip between Sebastian's eyes.

And Sebastian can see it. Clear as day. Watching as his stolen body bends and breaks in ways that should be impossible. Barreling through hails of blaster fire, unkillable. Ripping into human flesh with ragged, monstrous teeth. Trapped in his own head, unable to stop any of it. Unable to scream.

No. He can't think about that. Dammit. Focus.

He could beg for his life.

Sebastian's got a ton of pride. It's one of his best qualities, if he does say so himself. But one-on-one time with a sludge-brain is nothing if not a humbling experience.

He wonders how many humans have begged for their lives as Ringu dragged them off. Did its current host cry and snot up and plead as it infested her?

Begging won't get him very far.

"Confession time," he says. "I lied earlier. I am actually quite delectable. Umami like you wouldn't believe. We should really revisit the making-a-meal-of-me thing."

"Eating Se-ba-stian… Yun… wasteful."

"Oh, c'mon. Treat yourself. I can tell you're a hard-working creature of evil. You done earned yourself a tasty morsel, and I certainly won't go blabbing. C'mon. Gobble, gobble, nummy, nummy."

"Ever-y… day… listen-ing… to… Se-ba-stian… Yun… Every… day… wishing… we are… being… Seba-stian… Yun… Being… cool. This day… we are… doing."

"Wait, wait, wait!" Sebastian's mind scrounges up a recent memory. Something Buddy said. "You can't do this. Buddy—um, Hunter Find told us how it works with you sludgebrains. Your little hunting party don't get to take new hosts all willy-nilly. You gotta take me back to your hive and put it to a vote or whatever. I'm right, ain't I?"

Ringu nods. Sebastian gives himself a mental high five. He's getting out of here. There's still time.

"Long time… we are… thinking… Har-mony always… right. Even if… this Control… is not liking. Har-mony more… impor-tant… Then we are… listen-ing to… Se-ba-stian… Yun… Learning… better way… Se-ba-stian… Yun… way. This Control doing… what this… Control… is wanting."

Did this creature just say that Sebastian's bad influence inspired it to become a rule breaker?

"If you weren't a soulless body snatcher who preys on mankind, I'd swear Meza put you up to this."

His stomach tightens at the mention of her. His last, fleeting image of her flashes to mind.

No.

He can't afford to go there right now.

Ringu is talking to Sebastian. More talking equals more time not being infested by a sentient puddle of goo. Sebastian can talk. It's basically his whole thing.

"Let's think this through, Ringu. I can see the appeal of what you propose. I simply make being me look too daggone good. It's my curse. But you don't wanna be me—or like me, for that matter."

"Thinking... already. Deciding al-ready. Now... doing. Pre-paring."

Ringu turns away.

"No, hold up! You gotta have a look at all the facts first. There are things you don't know that you don't know. Look, this ain't for my sake. I'm only thinking of what's best for my biggest fan."

The sludgebrain pauses, glances over its shoulder.

Sebastian takes a breath and forces his body to relax. Pretends this is merely an episode of *So You Survived the End of the World*. Ringu is a caller and a loyal listener. It wants to hear what he's got to say.

Stretching out his legs, Sebastian leans back against the stalagmite behind him.

"I'd hate for you to have regrets, is all. I mean, this here's a big deal, right? Breaking your... Harmony's big, important rule. You might wanna hear me out before you go and do something you can't undo. But hey, if you'd rather reject my wisdom and take your chances, what's it to me?"

Ringu turns back, stares. As good an invitation to keep going as Sebastian figures he'll get.

"As I said, I know I make this whole being-me deal look glorious and easy, but some people are of the opinion that I'm going about life the entirely wrong way. And crazy as that sounds, they may be on to something."

"Se-ba-stian... Yun... perfect."

"It's hard to argue with that, but no." He only half fakes a pained expression as he pushes out the hardest words he has ever uttered. "I, Sebastian Yun, have got my flaws."

"Flaws?"

"That means I ain't as perfect as you and so many, many, many others think I am."

Ringu gasps. "Not... believing."

"Understandable, but you gotta trust ol' Bazzy here. I'd

never steer you wrong. You know that, right? It's why you listen to my show and find me so dang inspiring. Listen to me now. I. Ain't. Perfect."

It's mind-boggling, the lies that are born from desperation.

"How is Se-ba-stian… Yun… saying… this?" Ringu tilts its head, confused.

"Well, Ringu, let us rewind to earlier this very evening and the unpleasant woman with whom I was unfortunate enough to cross paths. She made quite a few crazy, outrageous statements about yours truly, which I flat-out rejected for the pile of dung it was.

"But now, finding myself in the predicament in which I find myself, I can't help but wonder if maybe she had it right about one or two things, and I just didn't want to hear it."

"What is she… saying?"

"First things first, allow me to set the scene. What you need to know is we were at this little Anti-Techer town. I didn't want to stop there, but Meza insisted. She wanted to try and trade with them or whatever, even though I said it was a terrible idea. I ain't never had an interaction with those loons that ended well.

"But I lost rock, dagger, blaster, so we stopped. The town leader came out with her whole posse. Blasters brandished, by the way. As if blasters ain't tech. But whatever. Since this was Meza's rodeo, I let her take the lead with these people, and, sure enough, she gets them to at least consider trading."

"Meza… is being… right. Always. Yes?"

"The story ain't done yet, thank you very much. So anyway, while Meza was talking to some skinny dude and this lady with a peg leg, the town leader brings her son over to me and points to me like I'm some exhibit and was all, 'Look at this cretin, Manny. This is why we reject technology and why our people will never listen to that little *music show* of his.'"

Sebastian's lip curls at the memory. She'd spat out "music show" like those words were a bad taste in her mouth. Otherwise, he might have been impressed that those Anti-Techers had heard of him at all. They aren't his target demographic.

Perhaps a passing caravan or some folk from the next nearest town mentioned him during trade visits. His reputation indeed precedes him these days.

"She was all like, 'This depraved individual has chosen to worship the corrupting machines of the past. For this, he has no people. No roots. And…'"

He hesitates to repeat the eerily prophetic part where she said that even Meza would abandon him one day. Not like he cares about something like that. Meza is free to go wherever she wants. Yet, for some reason, he skips past that bit.

"And nowhere to belong. Then she said, 'He will die alone —and soon. Is that what you want your life to be, son?' I could tell her kid wanted to say yeah, just to spite her. Being the good Samaritan I am, I gave poor Manny the means of getting his feelings out, with clear instructions to wait until morning before— That part ain't important.

"The moral of the story is that ol' battle ax, horrible as she is, did basically predict this. Not that I'm especially surprised. I ain't completely obtuse. I know that ultimately, I'm the only one I can count on. That is simply how things are out here.

"Still, can't help but think if I were a little better at going along with the program and not burning bridges, I woulda avoided meeting my inevitable and tragic fate quite so soon. It's too late for me, but you ain't lit any matches yet. You got your hunting pals and a nice home to go back to. You don't want to lose all that.

"So how's about you take me back to your friends and do this proper?"

Asking to be let go might be a bit of a stretch, especially considering that Sebastian's trying the let's-follow-the-rules approach. But going back to the others shouldn't be too big of an ask.

Plus, it takes him back to Meza. Who has to be okay because... because she's Meza, so of course she's okay. If there's one person in all of the Midlands who'd survive the odds he'd left her in, it's her. The overachiever.

"No." Ringu stalks away.

"No?" Sebastian repeats. "Just... no?"

"Prepare now. Se-ba-stian... Yun... mine."

At the dim edge of Sebastian's bubble of light, Ringu hunches double and digs into the earth like a dog. Which... huh?

Sebastian refuses to imagine the reason behind this odd behavior. Whatever the hole is for, he never wants to find out.

"Ringu, old friend, why no? Let's talk it out. Help me help you."

"No wasting... time. We are... digging now. Before... Hunters are... finding."

Well, yes, wasting time was kind of the point.

"With you taking over my body and all, you know you gotta take over my show, too, right? Reckon you're ready for that type of pressure? Fame ain't easy, I tell you what. Maybe I should show you the ropes first. Or what about a quick rundown of how I find music? The really good stuff. You wouldn't wanna waste your time on trash, right?"

It refuses to engage. Not good.

Sebastian casts a look about the cavern. It's hard to tell how big it is in the limited light, but the ceiling seems fairly high. However far away the walls are, the stalagmites are spread out pretty well. It isn't as cramped in here as it could be.

Keeping a wary eye on Ringu, he scans the surrounding area for something useful. But, alas, no one had the foresight to leave a bunch of blasters lying around for his convenience. Though wouldn't that have been nice?

Slowly at first, he inches around the cave, pulling his light with him. He checks over his shoulder constantly, but Ringu keeps at its digging. It doesn't even pause to look up.

Sebastian continues his search, moving farther and farther along until Ringu slips completely out of his sphere of light. He pauses, knowing that this will be the thing to bring the sludgebrain's wrath down on him.

The sound of Ringu's digging continues without interruption.

He keeps moving, but the best he finds is a good-sized rock. He picks it up and regards it glumly. Sludgebrain beats rock. He holds on to it anyway.

Getting a little bolder, Sebastian wanders steadily away from Ringu and the sound of digging.

He stumbles onto a large dark opening. His light fades down the wide tunnel. An exit?

This opening could lead anywhere. Including nowhere. But wherever it goes, it will be away from Ringu.

His feet carry him farther and farther from the sounds of digging until it fades away.

The path ahead is only as sure as the pool of light falling around his feet. The only right direction is the one taking him away from a future as a meat suit. The only sounds are the scraping of his feet against rock and the skittering of pebbles over the uneven ground.

It happens so gradually that Sebastian doesn't notice at first as the tunnel narrows. His shoulders almost brush the walls on either side of him. He doesn't travel the tight passage long before stepping into an expanse so wide Sebastian can't see the other side. Keeping the wall to one side, he continues on.

He wonders, uneasily, if he could stumble onto a sludge-brain hive. But he doesn't think so.

He still has no idea how far Ringu carried him from HRM to get to this cave system or how deep underground he is, but Ringu wants to keep Sebastian all to itself and safely away from others of its kind. It wouldn't bring him anywhere near its hive.

Or so Sebastian tells himself as he moves in the darkness.

He doesn't have much experience with caves, what with sludgebrains being underground before it was cool. But he knows enough to understand that they're dangerous even without monsters.

One wrong turn and he could plummet to his death or take himself deeper into the abyss instead of closer to the cave entrance, dooming him to wander until starvation or dehydration take him out.

And that's okay. Not a fun or glorious way to go. But it beats the alternative. He won't be a monster.

In fact, that's worth celebrating. And he has just the thing.

He tries to play music, but his cuff refuses to connect to the data stream. Too far underground.

Seriously? What's the point of curating an "About to Die" playlist if he can't play it when he's about to die? Talk about injustice.

Well, what else is there to do?

He intones the one-word opening chant of a song basically written for a moment like this, doing his best to capture the magic of five voices blending together in perfect harmony.

By the time he—very quietly, of course—comes to the end of "Crossroads", the wall he's following curves into another tunnel. This one becomes cramped with flat-topped rock formations so close to each other, he at times has to move sideways to slip through.

Stumbling into another open area, he thinks of Meza. Not that last sight of her, outnumbered by the monsters barreling down on her. That can't be the final picture of her he holds in his head.

He sings "Ready or Not" next. And not to be overly boastful, but he gives Lauryn Hill a run for her money. It really is a shame. All this time he should have been gifting the world with his melodious voice.

As he runs through the song, he sees Meza tinkering away at her messy side of the workbench. Focusing on the road from behind the wheel of HRM. Scowling at him.

Then, he lets himself think of Grace.

He doesn't feel like singing anymore.

For too long, the only footsteps he hears are his own. So he immediately recognizes when another set echoes down to him. They're sure steps. Too fast—and close.

Sebastian runs, stumbling over rocky obstacles.

Where is he running? Great question. He knows there's no escape for him down here. Ringu will catch up to him, and then it'll be over. Except it won't be. It'll be the start of a new nightmare.

How long do human hosts last as sludgebrains? Will it be five years of the hell to come? Twenty? Fifty?

Trick question. A single day as one of those things would be a day too long.

He sees it. It's hard to know for sure in the limited light, but yes… *yes!* As he runs toward it, he's sure the deep black patch in the ground ahead of him is the answer to his prayers.

He runs for the pit. Better to Thelma and Louise this than to allow himself to become a monster.

His stomach leaps into his throat as his foot plunges into nothing. Followed by the rest of him. One second he's running and in the next he's falling. But then, one second he's falling and in the next he isn't.

An indelicate, clawed hand has him.

Ringu drags him back and drops him to solid ground. The second he's free of the monster's grip, he dives back toward the pit. But Ringu's too fast. It catches him by the collar.

Sebastian drops, wriggling out of his jacket. He darts away, but Ringu catches him easily. The grip on his arm is unbreakable. He knows this because he tries to break it.

"Se-ba-stian... Yun... Not running. Yes?"

"You ain't exactly giving me a better option."

"Option. Not running. Option. Breaking... legs." It stabs at one of Sebastian's legs with a finger. "Legs mine... If breaking... this Control is... waiting for... healing... Not wanting."

"I'd hate to inconvenience you."

Ringu tosses Sebastian over its shoulder and speeds through the dark, back in the direction that they came. Sebastian has no idea how long he'd been wandering through the cave's shadows on his own. It had felt like hours, but within minutes—seconds, maybe—they're back in the cavern where they'd started.

Ringu stops next to its hole, which has gotten deep. Man-sized deep. It holds Sebastian up next to the hole, peers into the depths, looks Sebastian up and down, then reassesses its work. It looks entirely too pleased with itself.

"Yes. Good," it says.

Sebastian's pretty sure he can guess what that hole is for.

"Don't do this," he says, knowing it's futile.

Ringu holds him over the hole and lets go.

He lands with an "Oof!" but shakes off the stun of the

drop. Reaching out of the narrow, shoulder-height pit, he claws at the ground and scrabbles to pull himself out. The shaft's dirt walls crumble away under his feet.

With one hand, Ringu shoves one of Sebastian's arms back into the hole and pins him in place. It shovels dirt back into the hole.

"Seriously, you don't wanna do this. You're gonna regret this, man. No more dope tunes for you, and I reckon you don't wanna live in the world without my playlists. They're expertly curated." Sebastian's only half-aware of the gibberish spewing from his mouth as the hole fills at an alarming speed. Too soon, the dirt is up to his knees, then his waist.

"I'm scratching your name outta my dedication!"

Finally, only two parts of him remain unburied. His head and part of the arm wearing the data cuff. With the arm Ringu hadn't been holding down, Sebastian had made an attempt to scoop out the dirt trapping him. It was a pointless endeavor. In the end, most of that arm is buried too.

The glow from the holo-interface casts light at a strange angle. It adds distorting shadows to Ringu as it crouches down, face low to the ground. Sebastian watches in horror as silvery goop drips from every orifice of the host's face.

"Oh," Sebastian says. "That's… not… fun…"

The goop drops to the ground and inches toward Sebastian's exposed face.

"Not fun, not fun, not fun. No, no, no, no, no! No! No!"

The goop makes contact with his jaw. It spreads upward and brushes against his mouth.

"Gross. You didn't wash your hands."

He squeezes his mouth shut, but his eyes grow wide in panic. All bravado leaves him. This is happening. He's not getting out of this.

He drags air in and out too fast. Try as he might to slow his breathing, he can't control it. His head spins.

The goop prods at his mouth even as it extends more of itself up Sebastian's face. It spills into his nose, his ears, drips into his eyes. Squeezing his lids shut does nothing to stop it.

He whimpers, all pride gone. He's weak. He's alone. He's nothing. Desperation is all that's left of him as he finally allows his mind to go there, to picture what he is to become.

He begs.

"Just—Just kill me. Please."

But it's too late for that. Too late for anything but to fill his last human moments with screaming.

6

ALL AT ONCE, the aggressive pressure filling Sebastian's face lifts.

He coughs and gags as the silvery goop pulls away from him. It doesn't go easily. Tendrils of it cling to his nasal cavities, his eyelids, his tongue, his lips, to parts beneath his skin and his skull that he can't name.

Then he's free of the sludge. Completely.

And it makes no sense. How and why does he not have a new roommate in his brain?

Taking in shaky, gulping breaths, he blinks furiously until the blurry shadow crouched over him focuses into something he recognizes.

"We are finding first," Buddy says, looking the very picture of smug. "We are fastest Hunter. Fastest. Smartest. Best. Always. Hunters not believing. We are showing. Yes."

And God help him, Sebastian is happy to see the fiend. Euphoric, even.

This, to be clear, is a reflection of his state of mind. Not a sign of any growing attachment to the monster.

The odd lighting from the awkwardly angled cuff casts

Buddy in ghoulish shadows. Its long pale hair deepens the effect around its face. In one hand, it holds the squirming rogue sludge, which it draws close to its face.

"Very bad. Not following rules. Very big trouble."

"Get me out," Sebastian gasps. "Getmeoutgetmeout-getmeout!"

"Of course we are doing. We are helping."

"Help faster!" He squirms and pulls, but the packed dirt keeps its crushing grip.

"Stupid human. Very rude."

"Pardon me. Where are my manners? If you would very kindly, and at your own leisure, see fit to dig me out of this hellish pit, I would be ever so obliged. Please and thank you."

Buddy nods. "Mm. Much better. Sebastian Yun is holding."

"What?"

Buddy shoves the sludge into Sebastian's free hand.

Shocked, he takes it. Then his brain catches up with what has happened. He wretches. The wriggling thing in his hand is warm, muscly, and coated with a viscous slime.

"What!?!" Sebastian repeats.

"Holding tight. Not letting loose, yes? That Control. Very naughty."

He wants to drop it but stops himself, realizing that would give the sludge another opportunity to get clingy.

"Sure, I'll hold it real tight."

He tightens his fist into a death grip. He isn't sure what it takes to kill one of these things with one hand, but he's willing to find out.

Buddy snatches the sludge back. "No, not hurting that Control. Sebastian Yun is not being cool."

It presses the living wad of snot to its chest, coos at it in their nonaudible language.

"Sebastian Yun is killing every last one of you first chance he gets," says Sebastian Yun.

"Tch! Stupid human. We are holding, or we are digging. Not doing both. What is Sebastian Yun wanting?"

Sebastian glares up at Buddy, sure that the sludgebrain's idea of helping is taking him back to its friends. But playing along will at least get him out of this hole. Even if he'd rather stick his head between the gaping jaws of a hellion before agreeing to hold that thing again.

"Dig me out," he mutters.

"Sebastian Yun is holding. Tight, but not hurting."

"Yeah, yeah."

He opens his hand, and Buddy places the sludge in his palm. A shiver of disgust travels from the flesh of his palm and into every nook and cranny of his buried body.

Buddy proves to be an efficient digger. Watching it scoop out enormous clumps of dirt, Sebastian realizes it won't take long for it to free him. He presses his lips together and does his best to disassociate from the feelings of the slimy sludge in his hand.

The second he's free enough to move even an inch, he scrambles over Buddy, out of the hole, and away from the spot where his life as a human had almost come to a pitiful end.

Buddy leaps to its feet.

Sebastian takes another big step back. He holds the sludge high and over his shoulder, poised to throw it as hard as humanly possible.

"You can stay right there, thank you very much."

"What is stupid human doing? We are hurrying. Hunters are coming."

"This here is what we call a hostage situation. In case it ain't clear, your friend, the homicidal slug, is the hostage. That makes me the guy calling the shots. I'd love nothing more than to smash this thing into some especially sharp rocks, but seeing how it's worth something to you to keep it alive, I've found it in my heart to be merciful."

"We are not having time."

"What? You and your friends got somewhere to be?"

"They are not knowing we are helping. Very bad if they are finding."

"Helping," Sebastian scoffs. "As if you didn't lead them right to us. 'Cuz you know what I done figured out? Them names you sludgebrains got for each other ain't just names. They're jobs. You're like some kinda scout, ain't you, Hunter *Find*? You go ahead of the rest of them and find stray humans to round up. Tell me I'm wrong."

"Why are we saying Sebastian Yun is wrong? We are very good Hunter Find. Best."

"I can't believe Meza wanted to trust a thing like you. And it got her—" He can't bring himself to say she's dead. But how can it not be true?

Sure, sludgebrains prefer to drag their victims away. But there have been corpses found after an attack. Things happen. Some humans aren't worth the trouble of herding back to the hive. The ones who fight too hard, too smart. The ones who don't cower or give up. Humans like Meza.

"Trusting you ain't work out too well for her, did it?" Sebastian says.

"Meza is—"

"Don't say her name."

"Meza—"

The smart thing would be to keep his head and use his hostage to his advantage. But Meza might have been on to something about his lack of impulse control.

He lobs the sludge.

It sails over Buddy's head and disappears into the inky blackness.

"No!" Buddy races into the darkness.

Sebastian bolts to the entrance of the cavern. As fast as Buddy moves, he has zero time. Less than that.

Okay.

So, yes, that was stupid.

That was him literally throwing away the only leverage he had.

If he survives this, he'll start making better decisions.

Well…

Probably.

Maybe.

A figure appears suddenly in his sphere of light. Not believing his eyes, he trips over his feet in his attempt to stop and stumbles right into Meza. Simultaneously, she steps aside and reaches out to steady him. His flailing effort to remain upright brings them both down.

He manages to twist as he falls so that it's his back that slams into the rocky ground. She lands on top of him. All the air whooshes out of his lungs.

Centering himself amid all the confusion, he finds Meza's face staring down at him. Their noses are inches apart.

It's really her. And she's alive. Somehow. And here. Somehow.

"Hey," Sebastian says.

"Hey," Meza says.

"You're okay."

"Appears so."

He lets out a long breath. This time it has nothing to do with the wind being knocked out of him.

Meza goes still, and that's when he notices his hand cupping the side of her face, thumb running gently across her cheek. His hand freezes.

"Uuuuh…" he says, helpfully.

He pulls his hand back. The movement jolts them back to reality. They scramble apart and then to their feet.

"What're you doing here?" he asks.

"Out for a stroll."

"I mean, why are you standing alone in the dark?"

"Didn't much like the idea of this narrow exit being cut off if the other Hunters caught up. Stayed out here to keep watch while Buddy went after you."

He wants to ask about her coming down here with Buddy, but instead blurts, "You're keeping watch in the pitch-dark? Genius plan."

"Got ears, don't I? Believe it or not, some of us know how to shut up and listen."

"Fine. But we gotta go. Buddy ain't gonna be distracted long."

Sebastian pulls her along. Whatever its reason for bringing Meza along, they still can't trust Buddy. A monster is a monster. He'd rather not stick around to discover its ulterior motive.

Meza snatches her arm free. "What'd you do?"

"I bought us time. Which you are currently squandering."

"How quick you think we'll make it outta here without Buddy to guide us?" She returns to the tunnel opening. Leaning into the narrow entrance, she calls in a loud whisper, "Buddy. Whatever you're doing, hurry it up."

"You cannot be serious. You still trust that thing? It betrayed us! Literally, the second my back was turned."

"It was buying us time. It always intended to help us. You didn't hurt it, did you?"

"I wish."

"Buddy!" Her whisper is more urgent this time.

The sludgebrain appears out of the darkness like a wraith, and it looks none too pleased.

Sebastian tugs Meza away from the tunnel. Places himself between her and the angry monster.

The chivalrous move is wasted on her.

"Honestly," she says, sidestepping him, "if it wanted to hurt me, it had all the time it took for us to find you to do so."

"Sebastian Yun is lucky that we are liking Meza," Buddy says. "And that Scott is liking Sebastian Yun's show."

"Who the hell is Scott?"

Buddy's lips curl. "Tch. Stupid human."

"Sebastian, you have to trust it," Meza says.

"As far as I can throw it."

"Then trust me."

Sebastian opens his mouth to tell her exactly what he thinks about her judgment.

"Ain't asking," Meza says before he can get a syllable out. "I'm telling you. Rather take your chances with those other two when they track you?"

He narrows his eyes at Buddy. "I ain't turning my back on it."

"Whatever." She pulls Tennille from her waistband and Captain from a spare back holster she must have grabbed from HRM. But she pauses before handing them over. "Promised Buddy that if it helps us, we wouldn't try to kill its friends."

"Whyyyyyyyy would you make that sorta promise?" Sebastian asks.

"Something about needing to rescue you comes to mind."

"What about maiming and disfiguring? Are those still on the table?"

Meza hands both blasters over with a bland expression. Sebastian's heart fills with rainbows and unicorns as he embraces Captain and Tennille.

"Aw, did you miss Papa?" he croons lovingly. "Papa missed you too."

"Where's the one that carried him off?" Meza asks Buddy.

Buddy aims an accusatory look. "Sebastian Yun is hurting that Control very bad. We are having to put back in vessel. Healing. Taking very long time."

"I weep," Sebastian says.

"We ain't gotta worry about it coming behind us?" Meza asks.

"We are not worrying."

"That's something." Meza presses her lips together, then adds awkwardly. "But—um—Sorry about your friend."

Frowning, Buddy shuffles past Sebastian and Meza.

"Meza and Sebastian Yun are following. We are getting back to Her Royal Majesty. Fast. Before others are finding."

They follow. Sebastian scowls at Buddy's back. Meza's right. That sludgebrain is their best chance of making it back to HRM in one piece. They're at the mercy of this creature.

"The CGen?" Sebastian asks Meza.

"Dragged me out before I could finish the switch."

"Awesome. And this..." He gestures between Meza and Buddy. "How'd it happen?"

"After you were carried off, the redhead—"

"Carrie," Sebastian offers.

"And the big one—"

"Children of the Corn."

Meza gives him an "Are you done?" look.

"Corn for short," he adds, then gestures for her to proceed.

"The redhead and the big guy went off to bring you and the other one back. I was left with Buddy and the one with long arms—"

"Misery."

"Sebastian."

"Names are useful!"

"I gave Buddy the option to help me take down the one with the long arms and save you or let you take your chances with its friends. It chose you. For some reason."

Sebastian leans a little closer to whisper, "If this ain't a trick, why is it helping us?"

"Maybe it's a good guy." She doesn't bother to whisper.

"We are very good guy," Buddy says. "Best."

"Eat any humans lately?" Sebastian asks.

"Yes. Eating all the time. Very delicious."

"You really don't see anything wrong with what all you said, do you? Like, at all."

"Not wrong. Natural. Most natural. Control are best. Smartest, fastest, strongest. This is why we are being Control. Humans are hollow. Being what we want. Food. Vessels. All good."

Sebastian casts a meaningful look at Meza. "And this is who we're trusting with our very human lives. No way this ain't ending with some sludges wearing the latest in charming radio personality and plucky sidekick."

"Ain't your sidekick," Meza mutters.

"Vessels very lucky. Being made better than stupid, weak humans. Scott is knowing. Telling if you want."

"Who the hell is—"

"Scott is your host. Your vessel. Ain't he?" Meza asks.

"Why is Meza asking this? Meza and Sebastian Yun are meeting Scott already. Humans. Memories bad."

Meza's eyes widen. "When you came down from the bus earlier. That was Scott?"

"Mmh," Buddy says.

Sebastian exchanges a glance with Meza. Despite himself, he's intrigued.

"That normal?" Meza asks. "For a sludge to let the human take control back?"

Buddy hesitates before answering. "No. Not normal."

"Ain't no others like you, are there?"

"One day, Control are seeing. Doing better."

There's something wistful in its voice. Sad, Sebastian is tempted to think. But the last thing Sebastian is about to do is feel sorry for a sludgebrain.

"Right," he says. "A kinder, gentler parasitic monster. That'll be the day."

"We are helping Control see it. We are sharing *So You Survive End of World*. Hunters listening. Liking. Even though Sebastian Yun is stupid human. They are seeing. Humans are being cool sometimes."

"Is that really your brilliant plan? They hear a little music and next thing you know, sludges are letting their humans time-share their own bodies. Guess we'll have to see what happens when you introduce Scott to your friends."

Buddy stops suddenly. It spins around. "Meza and Sebastian Yun are not telling others, yes? Big trouble. Harmony Voice is punishing. Not forgiving. Bad. Very bad."

"I have so many chats with so many sludgebrains on such a regular basis. How ever will I keep this hot goss all to myself?"

"Sebastian Yun is not telling." Muscles bulking up, Buddy grows six inches taller in the blink of an eye. "This Control is not letting!"

Meza darts in front of Sebastian, raises her hands, placating. "He won't, Buddy. Swear. Sebastian forgets he ain't funny is all."

Buddy glares over her head at Sebastian, not quite mollified.

"You were joking, right?" Meza says.

"You know me. I keep 'em coming."

"Sebastian Yun is not telling?"

"How about you get us back to our ride and you never

have to worry about us running into you or anyone you know ever again? Both of us get what we want."

After a beat, Buddy nods. Slowly, it turns back and leads the way once again.

They move in silence for a long moment. Darkness behind them. Ahead, Buddy's dirt-streaked, bare back is lit by the holo-interface's blue glow.

"We are telling," Buddy says. "One day. Hunters good. Best. Hunters are understanding. Will work. Soon."

"What if you tell them about Scott and they don't understand?" Meza asks, ever curious about the life of this sludge-brain Sebastian has no intention of seeing ever again after this night.

"They are telling Harmony Voice."

"That's like your leaders or something, right?"

"Something like. Voice are keeping rules. Punishing bad Control."

"What kind of punishment they got for something like this?" Meza asks.

"Voice is taking vessel from us. Long time. Weeks. Months."

"They take your toy away?" Sebastian says. "Boohoo. Poor, wittle parasite."

"Not parasite. We are changing human vessel. Making better. Without Control, vessel is very sick. Dying."

"Scott wouldn't survive being separated from you," Meza interprets.

"Mmh. This is why we are sneaking. Helping humans. Very bad. Against rules. Big trouble. We are not risking Scott."

"However you try to spin it," Sebastian says, "still sounds like you ain't nothing but a nasty body snatcher to me. And maybe Scott would rather die than be your puppet a second longer. You ever think of that?"

"Stupid human is knowing nothing."

"Yeah? Why not let us ask him?"

Buddy says nothing.

"What're you afraid of?" Sebastian presses. "Unless you already know I'm right."

Buddy stops. Its proud shoulders round, and its spine curves just so as its head drops low.

"What's the holdup?" Sebastian says.

The sludgebrain turns around slowly, peering over its shoulder first before the rest of it follows.

"Hi." Buddy's eyes fall to its feet. The same as it did back at HRM before the other sludgebrains showed up.

"You're Scott," Meza says.

Scott nods.

"Very nice to meet you, Scott. Again."

"Very nice meeting."

Sebastian stares, stunned. "Well, hell. I didn't think it would really do it. Or… or is this another trick? It's a trick, right? Like, give this soulless puddle of goo an Oscar, amiright?"

Scott spins and continues forward. "We are walking. Very important. Saving Sebastian Yun and Meza."

It tosses a shy smile over its shoulder.

Sebastian regards the sludgebrain warily, but curiosity gets the better of him. He takes swift strides to catch up and place himself at Scott's side. "We heard what that thing in your head has to say, but how does all this really shake out for you?"

"Shaking… out?" Scott's expression shifts to understanding. "Oooh! Sebastian Yun is asking if Scott is being happy? Yes. Very happy. Buddy is Scott's best friend."

"But to be fair, how many friends you got?"

"I am having so many friends now! Buddy and Meza and

Sebastian Yun. More friends than ever before! Very so lucky!"

"That's— uh—" The saddest thing Sebastian has ever heard. And he's seen plenty of sadness in the Midlands. "That's right."

"Plus! Scott is having name!"

"I hate to break it to you, but everybody's got a name. That ain't a reason to send out the marching band."

"Control are not needing names. But when Scott is being very little, Buddy is asking name. Buddy is using name ever since because name is making Scott happy. See! Lucky!"

"How old were you when you were taken?" Sebastian asks.

Scott shrugs.

Had he been too young to know the answer to that question? Sebastian's stomach roils. Then he shakes off his pity. Feeling sorry for the kid won't do anything for him.

He jumps in Scott's path, bringing their progress to an abrupt halt.

"Let's cut to the chase. You ain't gotta live like a monster anymore. If you wanna be put out your misery, say the word. I'll make it happen."

Taking out this sludgebrain while it's leading them out of the cave doesn't sound like an especially great idea. And Sebastian firmly stands by his belief that martyrdom is a really dumb way to go.

But being turned into a monster is literally the worst thing that can happen to a person. A million times worse than just dying. Letting this kid suffer another day of this sorry excuse for a life… It's enough to inspire Sebastian to dust off his much neglected altruism.

He and Meza can figure a way out of this mess. This might be Scott's only chance to be free from this nightmare.

Scott takes a step back, eyes wide. "Sebastian Yun is not hurting Buddy. Buddy is Scott's best friend."

The sludgebrain steps around Sebastian and continues forward.

Sebastian shakes his head. "I don't understand No, wait. *You* don't understand. You got that Stockholm syndrome they talk about in Old World movies."

"We are having… stock… home…?" Scott asks, trying out the shape of the unfamiliar word.

"I'll break it down for you. You're human. Or were. Even if you don't remember it, humans are your people. Monsters are not your people. They're the enemy of all humanity. And Buddy is the evil monster who stole your body.

"Humans—like me, like Meza, like you if you knew any better—would rather die than live as monsters. If that goop hadn't got into your head and scrambled everything up, you'd know that. Hell, you'd feel how wrong this is down to your core. Back me up, Meza?"

Meza says nothing. Her face is stone.

"C'mon, Meza!"

Scott pauses and looks from Sebastian to Meza, brows furrowed as if working out the interlocking pieces of a puzzle. On this, Sebastian is on the same page as the sludgebrain. Of all times for Meza to go all silently stoic.

"Sebastian Yun is not getting," Scott says. "Buddy is Scott's people. Most important. Like Meza is being most important to Sebastian Yun. Happy together. Yes? Because Meza is Sebastian Yun's people."

Sebastian glances at Meza, then away again. "Well, I mean, that ain't exactly how I would describe our—um… association. But when did this become about me and Meza? We're talking about you being brainwashed into thinking anything about your situation is okay."

"Scott is not saying everything is okay. Control are

thinking humans are nothing. Treating humans bad. Very, very bad. Treating new vessels worst. Control are... they are..."

Scott searches for the right word.

"Breaking! They are breaking humans. And if—if new vessels are being very young, very believing... Sometimes what Control is thinking is funny is not being funny at all."

A shadow crosses the sludgebrain's face, perhaps recalling some particular memory better left unstated.

"Great speech," Sebastian says. "You really done convinced me."

"Buddy is being different. Very cool. Never mean. Letting Scott run and jump. Talking. We are talking. Always. Being very safe. Secret. Buddy is Control but is not choosing. Just is. But Buddy is making decision. Being good guy. Helping Sebastian Yun and Meza because Sebastian Yun and Meza are important to Scott. That is why Scott and Buddy are being friends."

A good body-snatching parasite? A happy-to-be-along-for-the-ride host?

Impossible. Flat-out. No way. The end. Final answer.

"This is ridiculous," Sebastian says. "You can't be happy. Just because the nice mind-controlling monster that—I'm sure—stole you away as a child sometimes lets you take a ride in your own body don't mean you're lucky. Maybe if you got a chance to grow up a real human, you'd know how wrong it is for you to be sticking up for the thing that ain't never gave you a choice in becoming a filthy sludgebrain—"

"Sebastian, stop." Meza's tone is even but firm. "He's fine."

"How can you say that? Nobody in that situation—" He waves a hand at Scott. "—is fine. And for the record, Meza, because you apparently are the only human being on the planet who needs to be told this. If I get turned into a monster, you better not hesitate to kill me. I refuse to live as something like that."

She wheels on him. "Why can't you see that this whole monster thing ain't as black-and-white as you think?"

"That is literally the dumbest thing I ever heard. And I done listened to every William Shatner album in existence."

Scott shakes his head, distressed. "We are not liking this. Buddy is coming back. Yes?"

The sludgebrain's back straightens and its shoulders square. Buddy hefts its chin and looks down its nose.

"Sebastian Yun is seeing. Yes?"

"No, Sebastian Yun is not seeing."

He has never understood anything less. Not Buddy, not Scott, and definitely not Meza. He's tired of this cave, this darkness, and being the only sane person he knows.

7

THEY TRUDGE along in the blue glow of Sebastian's light. Meza and Buddy are both wordless. Not that he cares if the sludgebrain ever speaks to him again. But Meza's silence nags at him.

He'd gotten used to the taciturn side of her personality—or so he believed. But she'd been acting so weird earlier without bothering to explain herself. True, she's never exactly been an open book. Turns out, he understands her even less than he'd thought.

He sighs. "I feel bad."

"Doubtful," Meza says.

"I mean it! You realize that the next time I get terrorized by psychotic sludgebrains who also happen to be my biggest fans, you won't be around for the fun. I'm really sorry that you're gonna miss out."

"However does one manage in this world without your particular brand of chaos?"

"You ain't gotta be brave for me. I know the thought of not being around for future adventures is tearing you apart on the inside. But you ain't got nobody to blame but yourself."

She only offers a "Hm." And a lackluster one at that.

Sebastian absently drums his fingernails on the side of his Devastator. A soft, rapid *taptaptaptap* against metal.

"I'm throwing you a going-away party," he says. "Next town we get to, assuming they ain't a bunch of Anti-Techers, of course. Music, food, booze. So much booze. And games! Yes, definitely games. One of them, I'm calling Mezapoly. Don't know how to play it yet, but I'll figure it out. I'ma see you off in style, Miss Meza. Yes, sirree."

She doesn't respond to this declaration at all.

"And look, I know you're gonna pine for my incomparable company as well as the comforts of Her Royal Majesty, and you'll regret your decision to give up all of this just so you can live an exceptionally long yet predictable life, but it's gonna be okay, Meza. That aching void in the core of your being may never go away, but I reckon you'll find a way to cope. Eventually."

"Give it a rest, Sebastian. I ain't going nowhere."

"Don't go changing your mind on my account."

"Never said I was leaving."

"Yeah, you did. You were all…"

Sebastian thinks back. What had her exact words been? It had definitely been something about leaving. Or…

He replays the conversation from earlier this evening. They'd been tearing down the road with those Anti-Techers on their heels. She'd been chewing him out about impulse control or whatever. He'd reminded her that life is too short for all that worry she carries around.

And she said—

Hmm…

All she'd said was, *"What am I doing here?"*

Then, he'd interpreted that as her saying she wanted to leave.

And here, he might have to consider that maybe that bitter hag of a town leader had gotten into his head. Just a little tiny bit.

Well, it isn't so crazy that he'd leapt—arrived—at that perfectly reasonable conclusion. People leave. It's simply what they do. Whether of their own volition or not.

And Meza made no effort to correct that assumption until now.

"And you let me go on thinking you were packing it up?" Sebastian asks.

"Now you want me to step in when you decide to make a fool of yourself?"

He presses a hand to his chest, feigning offense. "I was gonna throw you a party."

Perhaps there'd been a small amount of jumping to conclusions on his part, but Meza had let him believe that she intended to leave. She had been mad.

Despite that, she'd come after him. Even though it meant striking a deal with a sludgebrain who, by all appearances, betrayed them and then diving headfirst into this dark and endless cave.

He should have been lost. Another casualty of this monster-filled world.

But she'd come after him.

"So you're sticking around?" he asks.

"I'm sticking around."

"Good. I mean, if that's what you want."

They lapse into silence again, but this time it doesn't bother him.

"You all feel that?" Sebastian asks.

A subtle shift in the atmosphere. Fresh air. The entrance

to the cave must be somewhere near. Almost of their own volition, his steps quicken.

"We're nearly out of this hellscape."

Buddy freezes, turns back to Sebastian and Meza with alarm written across its face.

Then Sebastian feels it.

While wandering the cave, he'd taken some sliver of comfort in the fact that the other Hunters couldn't have been that close. As long as he didn't feel the Dissonance.

But now the familiar and unwelcome sensation fills his head.

"We got to—"

Buddy clamps a hand over Sebastian's mouth.

Before his disgust can fully register, he is hefted up then slung over the sludgebrain's shoulder. Suddenly, they're in motion. His shadowed surroundings merge into one dark blur.

Then they're still, and Sebastian's on his own two feet again.

They're outside the cave. Compared to the inky black they'd just left, the night is full of light. The stars above, distant and indifferent as they are, provide a welcome change from the claustrophobic cave. Moonlight paints the edges of the towering rock formations in silver.

Teetering on shaky legs, Sebastian's eyes fall on Buddy, then he springs back. He chokes out something between a shriek and gasp.

His uncertain balance not quite up to the unplanned motion, he starts to fall. Buddy reaches out a grotesque hand to keep him upright.

Sebastian recoils from the touch.

Up until that moment, Buddy's appearance had remained more or less that of a human. A gross, dirty human walking around buck naked, but it made being near Buddy so long almost tolerable.

But now, it's gone full monster.

Legs stretched and bent backward for speed. Muscles bulked out with sinews drawn in exaggerated relief. Face contorted into harsh planes that erase its boyish features. Mouth wide and exposing rows of jagged teeth.

It puts a long, clawed finger to its lips. "Remembering. If we are hearing Hunters, Hunters are hearing us."

Swallowing a bit of bile, Sebastian manages to not scream. Instead, he hisses, "Meza!"

Buddy is a streak of motion darting back in the direction they'd come. Sebastian turns off his holo-interface and scans his rocky surroundings.

In the distance, brightness peeks above the stone giants crowding the landscape. With a jolt of surprise, Sebastian realizes that light must be from HRM. How much distance had Buddy covered when it carried him out of the cave?

The distant glow beckons. A guiding light in the storm. Her Royal Majesty reaching out to him across the night. He races toward it.

When Buddy returns with Meza, it smoothly deposits her at Sebastian's side. She's running with him the second her feet touch uneven ground.

"We are giving Sebastian Yun and Meza little time only. Hunters catching up. Very soon." Buddy speaks at a normal volume. It must not hear the other Hunters.

"Ain't no way we're outpacing them," Meza says.

"Buddy, you gotta run Meza on ahead."

"No, you—"

Sebastian cuts off Meza's protest. "Ladies first, I insist."

"Thought you didn't like martyrs."

"Ain't being a martyr or a gentleman here. You get there first, finish fixing the CGen lickety- quick. Buddy can—" His entire being rejects the thought of willingly letting a sludgebrain carry him off. He's had enough of that for a lifetime. "Buddy can come back for me."

"Okay." Meza throws herself into Buddy's arms.

They disappear between the rock formations. As fast as Buddy moves, Sebastian might as well be standing still. He keeps running, for what it's worth.

Turns out it's not worth much. He's been alone for all of a few minutes when the Dissonance presses against the inside of his skull.

Out of time.

Will Buddy bother coming back for him?

All night, it's been sneaky about aiding Sebastian and Meza. With the other Hunters near, Buddy won't risk helping outright.

Buddy reappears so suddenly that Sebastian nearly collides into it. They regard each other warily, both unsure of what's about to happen. The Dissonance is pounding.

Head strung low, Buddy meets Sebastian's eyes. It pleads, wordlessly. Begs him to play along. Then it raises its head and throws a silent whistle greeting over Sebastian's head. At the sludgebrains who have, at last, caught up.

Run.

Fight.

Do anything but go down easy.

Every instinct within Sebastian—instincts honed from a lifetime of surviving a world out to extinguish the human race—rails against the decision he's already made. The worst of all options.

To trust a monster.

He grits his teeth, but doesn't resist when Buddy tears away his weapons and tosses them aside. It pushes him to face the other Hunters. Its grip remains on his shoulder, tight enough that its claws press into his skin.

Children of the Corn and Carrie radiate distrust as they

stalk closer. On its back, Carrie holds Ringu. The dark-haired sludgebrain has seen better days. Having reverted to a form that's mostly human-looking, it slumps against Carrie. Sebastian can't be sure it's conscious until it groans and its head lists groggily to the side.

Hmph. Serves it right. Try infesting somebody now.

Not that Sebastian's in a position to take a victory lap.

The sludgebrains talk to each other. Though, of course, Sebastian can't hear a thing. To him, it looks as though someone pressed mute on the most tense moment in a movie. A horror flick, naturally.

The Dissonance presses into his head like a physical thing, and he realizes what causes that sensation. Whatever frequency the sludgebrains talk to each other on, humans are sensitive to it, even if they can't hear the sound.

It also explains why the Dissonance isn't completely reliable for predicting a pending sludgebrain attack. It's simple, really. Sometimes the monsters are talking to each other as they gear up for an attack, and sometimes they aren't.

Sebastian pushes away the revelation. It's not the most useful piece of information at the moment.

He focuses on the monsters before him, their body language. The challenge is to not see them as wild, danger-ous, unthinking animals. They're wild, dangerous, *thinking* animals. That communicate with more than just their words.

He can guess that Buddy is singing the same old tune. "Looky how I tricked the stupid humans into trusting me again."

From their rigid stances and shuttered expressions, Corn and Carrie aren't buying it so easily this time. Sebastian glances at his weapons, only a few strides away. But the sludgebrains will never let him reach them.

Trusting a monster. Did he really just willingly leave his fate up to Buddy's acting chops?

Corn gestures angrily to Sebastian and then to Ringu. Ringu attempts to lift its head, but it only amounts to a lethargic lolling. As ever, tangles of black hair obscure its face, but another low groan spills out from behind the dark curtain.

Buddy's grip on Sebastian's shoulder tightens. It grows more animated. Making some kind of argument, Sebastian fills in. Corn grows more animated, too, taut with anger that simmers close to the surface, threatening to boil over.

Carrie puts a hand up between the two. Playing the mediator.

Sebastian eyes his blasters again. Yup, still on the ground instead of snuggly in his hands where they'd be of some use.

This exchange between the sludgebrains isn't going well.

Sebastian weighs the merits of them exploding into a big brawl amongst themselves.

Would that give him the opportunity to slip away? Or would he be shredded to a million pieces, considering he'd be standing center of the action when they start throwing claws?

Assuming he can duck and roll fast enough to get clear, a sludgebrain throw down could be to his favor. Divide and conquer, and finally get the hell out of this creepy valley.

He's been known to have an aggravating effect on people, why not sludgebrains too?

Corn stabs a finger at Sebastian again. Carrie reaches for him, but Buddy jerks him back.

He's a part of this argument whether he wants to be or not.

"What's going on?" he asks.

They ignore him.

"What're they saying?" Sebastian asks Buddy, then addresses the group in general. "What're you all saying?"

They continue to pretend he isn't speaking. So rude.

Sebastian pops his pinkies in his mouth and whistles. The shrill sound works as intended.

All sludgebrain attention centers on him.

Yay.

"I know y'all understand what I'm saying, and I know y'all can talk in my language. Let's remember manners and speak so all relevant parties can participate in the conversation."

Corn, who seems super jazzed to have its important monster business interrupted by a mere human, hunches to bring its face even with Sebastian's. It oozes predatory intent.

"Re-le-vant?" Children of the Corn growls. "Silly human? No. Not… re-le-vant. But… we are… curious. These Control listen-ing to… Se-ba-stian… Yun… Every day. Now these Control…" Its brooding gaze shifts to Buddy, to Ringu, then back to Sebastian. "Acting… strange. Acting… wrong. Why… Se-ba-stian… Yun?"

He puzzles over if that's supposed to be "Why, Sebastian Yun?" or "Why Sebastian Yun?"

Not that he'd have an especially satisfactory answer either way. So he offers the only response he can.

"What can I say?" He shrugs. "Some of us are born with a talent for influencing the masses. Yes, it is a heavy burden, but I carry it well, wouldn't you agree?"

Corn growls, a low grumble in the back of its throat.

"But is this really about me? My question is where do these two get off?" He flaps a hand toward Buddy and Ringu. "Here you are, trying to do your job. Hold things together. Collect a few humans to take home to Mom and Dad. And here comes these guys, flying off the handle."

Buddy's hand clenches on Sebastian's shoulder, the claws digging into his flesh without breaking skin. A warning. He ignores it.

"You're obviously the leader, and clearly very good at it, might I add. But these two here refuse to toe the line.

Straight up disrespect is what I'm seeing. The question is, what are we gonna do to resolve this crisis of confidence? How're we gonna remind them who's boss?"

Corn grins, and it's the ugliest thing Sebastian has ever seen. "Se-ba-stian… Yun… dying."

"Other than that."

"We are not acting wrong," Buddy says. "We are only thinking, maybe we are letting Sebastian Yun go. We are all listening to Sebastian Yun. Liking music, yes? Laughing at stupid human, yes? Sebastian Yun is going. We are having music and laughing. Hunters are wanting, yes?"

Corn's lips contort into a whistle that Sebastian can't hear.

"What did it say?" Sebastian asks.

"We are say-ing," Corn snaps, "human… music… not… import-ant. That Control… import-ant. Very hurt. Needing healing. Needing food. Se-ba-stian… Yun… Not… import-ant."

No question who the food is in this scenario. Ringu stares at Sebastian like it's seeing an anthropomorphic, cartoon ham. So that's a pretty good clue.

"We are getting another human," Buddy says. "Very fast. Fastest."

"Human… here…"

Corn slips back into the sludgebrain language, the movements of its lips rapid and clipped.

"We are not loving humans!" Buddy cries. "Loyal. Always. We are loving Control."

A snarl rips across the valley. It's not from any of the sludgebrains pinning in Sebastian.

He searches for the source of the sound. It comes from the direction of HRM. On a squat rock formation a short distance away, the sludgebrain with long arms and the face of a middle-aged woman drags itself to standing.

Hands pressing into the surface of the rock, Misery leans heavily on its arms. It's splattered with something dark. Blood? Its own, Sebastian guesses.

Radiating fury, it points a long finger down at the group. No. At Buddy. It whistles something.

Sebastian has lost whatever thread of conversation he'd been grasping at. But things are not looking good when Children of the Corn and Carrie turn back to Buddy in horror.

They all start talking and gesturing at once. Sebastian struggles to keep up with the rapidly shifting gestures and body language. His eyes catch on Ringu, leering out from behind its curtain of dark hair.

Its fixed stare is worlds different than before, when it had wanted to possess Sebastian. This stare is hungry. In the literal sense.

In a sudden burst of energy, it springs over Carrie's shoulder.

Sebastian springs back. Raises his arms to cover himself. He knows his flimsy flesh and bones will be nothing against those razor teeth and wicked claws.

He lurches. But it's not from a ravenous sludgebrain pouncing on him. After yanking him out of Ringu's trajectory, Buddy tosses Sebastian indelicately to the side.

Side stinging from the rough landing against rocks, Sebastian twists in the dirt to reorient himself. And catches the sight of Ringu tearing a bloody chunk out of Buddy's arm.

Sebastian grimaces. Those ferocious teeth had been meant for him. It would have been fatal. Buddy only falters a little. It reaches around and pulls the dark-haired sludgebrain off him.

Ringu doesn't have much fight left in it. Whatever burst

of energy it found fades quickly. Its weak thrashing doesn't hold much threat for Buddy.

Then Misery is there. It launches itself onto Buddy, furious claws flying. Carrie jumps in, attempting to pull Misery away. It's a scene of bloody chaos.

Being in the middle of a sludgebrain brawl would not have been good. Not even a little. But this is the chance Sebastian had been waiting for. He sidles toward his weapons. All the while praying for invisibility like it's the only thing on his Christmas list to Santa.

The Dissonance spikes in his head. All the sludgebrains drop to the ground, clamping their claws to their ears and writhing in the dirt.

Only one monster remains standing. It towers over the others. Mouth stretched and neck muscles straining, it unleashes a silent roar on the others.

This is like what happened before. When Misery had subdued Buddy. But it's so much more. All the sludgebrains are crushed. Utterly. They can't even fight back. This is why they call the big guy Hunter Shriek.

Sebastian picks his jaw off the ground and remembers those blasters of his. Casting off caution, he dives for the weapons.

The second his fingers land on Captain, he swivels to face the last sludgebrain standing.

In that same instant, said last sludgebrain standing seems to remember who it blames for all this. Corn twists toward Sebastian and lunges, all teeth and claws and wrath.

Sebastian fires.

Corn swivels midpounce.

The shot is off. Instead of getting the sludgebrain in the head, it's a chest shot. Close range.

Children of the Corn goes down for a nap.

A few paces away, Carrie stirs weakly. The small movement reminds Sebastian that these sludgebrains are down but not out.

Time to fix that.

Sebastian leaps to his feet and takes aim at Corn. No way he's missing the head. Not this time.

His finger tightens on the trigger, but he's knocked off-center. The shot goes wide, and he falls.

Sebastian scrambles out from Buddy's hold. Its weak tackle—really, gravity had done most of the work—had made him miss the easiest shot in the world. He stops himself from aiming Captain's barrel between Buddy's eyes. But only just.

"Seriously, dude! Pick a side."

A feral snarl rips from Buddy. It bares rows of jagged teeth, eyes wild.

Sebastian swallows. "Or don't. Do you."

"Run," Buddy growls.

Sebastian, for once, is happy to be in agreement with a sludgebrain. Only barely remembering to snatch Tennille from the ground, he runs.

8

SEBASTIAN FLINGS himself across the rocky and uneven landscape. Pure adrenaline gets him over protruding stones and around craggy pillars at neck-breaking speed.

Buddy's urgent "Run" echoes in his head. A looming threat.

He skids to a stop, or tries to, but can't avoid slamming front first into a wall of rock blocking his path.

It's too high to climb quickly. He frantically skirts the wall, running his hands across the striated rock. No human-sized openings reveal themselves.

The multiple jutting and lopsided columns might as well be one gargantuan stony slab for as impassable as they are. The neighboring formations are even taller and more wall-like.

Of course it would be nothing for a sludgebrain to scrabble over this, even carrying a person, as Buddy had been. Sebastian is only human.

He kicks at the rocks. How dare nature put this giant obstacle in the middle of his escape route?

Then, he holsters Captain, flings himself at the formations ahead of him, and climbs. Time isn't a luxury he can spare.

He hurls a slew of insults at the obstruction, at Buddy for making him spare the sludgebrains that are sure to be on him any second, at Manny for not following simple, freakin' commonsense instructions. His outpour of insults becomes increasingly creative with each inch he rises.

He's a quarter of the way up when he notices a gap. The jutting of rock beneath it had hidden the opening from view. The crevice is barely wide enough for him to scrape through. He'll only be able to go so fast, and that's assuming the slim gap doesn't narrow to impassibility.

Sinister visions rush to him.

A sludgebrain meeting him on the other side, mouth open wide and welcoming. One of those monsters slithering in after him with the way before him blocked. Giving him nowhere to go.

He invents a whole new class of swearing as he removes his holsters. With Captain in one hand and the straps of his holsters in the other, he squeezes sideways into the crevice.

The rough, unforgiving rock snags his clothes and scrapes against exposed skin. In the tight space, his heartbeat thuds in his ears. Forcing his breaths to remain even, he tells himself that craggy walls are not getting closer. Unless they are. He won't get stuck. Unless he does. There is an opening on the other side. Unless there isn't.

Suffocating here is still a million times better than being body snatched and infested. So… winning?

He tumbles out the other side through a sawtooth opening that is definitely slighter than the opening he started through. His skin stings with fresh scrapes, a parting gift from the crevice.

But he can see the bridge, and part of HRM. Her lights

draw him. His home base in the world's worst game of hide-and-seek.

The way forward is lined with walls of rock on both sides but otherwise wide and unobstructed. He simply has to make it up a sloping incline.

He's already out of breath, but he slings his holsters back into place and races toward the promise of safety.

Stupid nature. Putting an incline in the middle of his escape route.

Then he senses it. Right behind him. Gripping Captain in both hands, he whips around.

Before he can take aim, before he even truly spots which sludgebrain has caught up to him, blaster fire lights up the night. The shots arc clear over his head and strike the sludgebrain not ten feet behind him.

Snarling, Corn stumbles. It's bleeding and battered but in remarkable shape for something that had taken a close-range shot from a Devastator not five minutes ago.

Sebastian spins back in the direction from which the fire had come.

It's Meza, of course.

Amazing, wonderful, stupendous, helluva-shot Meza.

She's perched on a collection of boulders that butt against the bridge. Her form and the Devastator pointed into the valley are outlined by the silver light of the moon. She gives a small tilt to her head, which Sebastian translates to "Take your time."

"You think I'm out for a stroll?" he quips back, as if she can hear him.

He does not take his time, what with his fondness for being alive. The darkness strobes with the flashing of her cover fire as he runs.

He's more than halfway up the incline when a shadow

drops down onto Meza's boulder. Sebastian screams a warning.

The cover fire stops suddenly as Meza spins to face Misery. The sludgebrain shoves the blaster's barrel away and darts in for the kill.

There's a short, confusing struggle, then both human and monster tumble down. They fall somewhere between the boulders where Sebastian can no longer see them.

Heart already bursting, Sebastian picks up speed. He knows there's nothing he can do for her. She's too far away. But he runs.

Corn crashes directly into his path. Sebastian skids to a halt so abruptly, his legs fall out from under him.

The hulking sludgebrain is on all fours. Even so, it looms over Sebastian. Head low to the ground, it stalks forward with a growl in its throat.

This isn't the impassioned monster that had earlier put Sebastian and Meza in their place then promptly forgot about them. Pure hatred fills Corn's eyes. As far as it's concerned, this is all Sebastian's fault.

Which, as far as Sebastian is concerned, is totally unfair.

It's not as if he started *So You Survived the End of the World* with the specific agenda of suborning sludgebrains. What are they doing even listening to his stupid human show?

If he'd known it would lead to this, he'd have included a disclaimer at the start of each broadcast: *Not intended for consumption by soulless, body-snatching monsters of pure evil. Listen at your own risk.*

Sebastian raises his Devastator. Corn lunges with a bone-shaking roar.

Then Buddy is there.

Being carried by a sludgebrain should be a familiar sensation to Sebastian by now.

It is not.

He will never get used to it.

At least this time, it's a short trip.

Seconds later, Sebastian finds himself off the main throughway, if the wide path up the valley can be called that. Buddy shoves Sebastian into a shallow alcove ten feet up a cliff face and plants itself in front of it.

Corn is super happy about this development.

It clambers up the rock wall and joins Buddy on the natural ledge attached to the alcove.

Sebastian shoves his back against the craggy cavity wall and raises his Devastator. This is going to be bad. Corn is in the mood for murder, and with one shriek, Buddy will be down. Sebastian will have nowhere to run.

Buddy raises its palms and shrinks down to its human appearance. Lowering its head, it whistles something at Corn.

Corn opens its mouth and shrieks, but it's a short outburst. Over as quickly as it starts. Buddy recoils like it's been slapped but remains on its feet. It makes no move to retaliate or fight back.

Glaring down at Buddy, Corn huffs and puffs like it's working its way up to breathing fire. Then, all at once, its bluster deflates. It regards Buddy with a mixture of confusion and sadness and… something else.

It gives a short, silent whistle.

Somehow, without understanding or even hearing their language, Sebastian understands what Children of the Corn is asking.

Why?

It watches Buddy with such heartbreak that Sebastian feels for Corn. Or, at least he would've. Were he capable of feeling any sympathy for a vile creature that wants to feed him to its friend after that friend attempted to turn him into a nightmarish monster.

But Sebastian isn't that evolved.

Buddy, however, crumbles under Corn's naked anguish. Shoulders arching, it responds in the sludgebrain language. Sebastian gets the impression that it's speaking slowly, cautiously. Its eyes fall to the ground and lock there.

Shame.

Meanwhile, Corn's face shifts through a gamut of expressions. First, its brows furrow with deepening confusion. Then, its eyes widen with surprise. Finally, its face turns stony, unreadable.

Buddy's gaze remains trained on the ground and mired in its own turmoil. It's completely oblivious when Corn's demeanor switches to something dangerous.

Corn says something short and perfunctory, then turns that terrible expression on Sebastian.

Sebastian flinches back. "I didn't do it!"

The words come out on reflex, but to his surprise, Corn replies.

"Yes… Se-ba-stian… Yun… is doing. Making… Hunter Find… weak… con-fused…"

"I ain't got a clue what it's been saying and, really, whatever this is feels like a private matter, not meant for mixed company. So you know what, how about I see myself out?"

Sebastian inches to the side, but one snarl from Corn freezes him midstep.

"Or I can set a spell."

"Sebastian Yun is not doing," Buddy says. "We are—"

Carrie drops in at Corn's side, Ringu once again on its back. Its audience growing, Buddy hunches, making itself smaller. But it continues.

"We are thinking these things already. Only now saying. Being… brave."

"Being brave?" Corn's lip curls in disgust. "Saying… we

are… treating humans… bad. Saying we… are needing… to… be bet-ter. Saying… Control are… wrong."

Corn shakes its head. Sebastian is baffled. It's almost as if, despite its disgust, Corn is really trying to understand Buddy.

"Why… is Hunter Find… saying these… things? How?"

"Be—Because…" Buddy looks from Corn to Carrie, then back to the ground. It's cornered itself. Even standing directly at its back, Sebastian barely hears it say, "Because… Scott—"

"Scott?" Corn says evenly. Too evenly. "Another… human…"

A horrible feeling sinks in Sebastian's gut. A really, really, *really* horrible feeling.

Despite boasting of being a member of the superior species, Buddy does something incredibly dumb. It's some-thing that the stupid human behind it, if asked, would have said belongs in the book of record-breakingly bad ideas. Right there next to New Coke.

But the stupid human is not consulted. Nor is the human listened to when said human warns, "Uh… Buddy, maybe now ain't the—"

"Human. Yes." Buddy presses a hand to its chest. "This human. And being friend."

Oh, the awkwardness! Sebastian very much wishes he weren't here for this. In fact, it's quite possible that he's never wanted anything more.

Corn and Carrie both start whistling at once. From what Sebastian can tell, it's far from a rally of support. Gesturing wildly, they both seem to grow taller as Buddy shrinks.

"Yes. We are talking to Scott. We are not wrong. Not wanting punishment." Buddy talks fast, words racing to keep up with the barrage from Corn and Carrie. "No. No. Hunters are seeing. We are better talking. We are having… having harmony. Real harmony. Not wrong. M-maybe Voice is wrong. Not this Control. We are loving Control. Always. We are wanting better. We—we are showing! Hunters are seeing. Trying, yes?"

"Wait," Sebastian says, realizing what Buddy is about to do.

But Buddy stands straighter, meeting its fellow Hunters' eyes. Defiant. Sebastian knows a lost cause when he sees one. Unfortunately, Buddy does not.

It really believes it can change these monsters.

Of all the sludgebrains to be reliant on to get out of this alive, Sebastian is stuck with the delusional one.

"We are helping Hunters understand. Hunters are meeting Scott."

Buddy's posture changes, what Sebastian now recognizes as the telltale shift of control from sludge to human. Scott folds inward, body rigid.

"Bad idea," Scott mumbles, barely audible. "Bad idea. Bad idea."

It's clear who's the brains in this relationship.

The sludgebrain's shoulders straighten. "Come, Scott. Scott is trusting this Control, yes? This Control is trusting Hunters. Friends. Saying hello, yes?"

Scott reemerges, stares at the ground as if willing a sinkhole to open. "H-Hello. Nice meeting."

Buddy either has more faith in its friends than they deserve, or it's dug itself into a pit of trouble so deep that it doesn't know what else to do but to keep tunneling until it reaches rock bottom.

Whatever the case, the other sludgebrains' reaction to this revelation cannot be what it had been hoping for.

First, there's a moment of stillness, like a held breath. In this short stretch of seconds, Corn and Carrie don't seem to understand what they're seeing. Or perhaps it's straight-up denial.

Ringu is also still. But that hardly counts. The creature is so out of it that it probably wouldn't know if the world came to an end. Again.

It does, however, manage to keep its hungry stare pointed at Sebastian.

And Sebastian, not being a stupid human but actually a pretty smart human—when it counts, at least—does three things almost simultaneously.

1. Estimates the remaining distance between him and HRM.
2. Eyes the quickest and most efficient way out of this alcove and back down to the wide path to the bridge.
3. Discreetly activates his holo-interface and opens a recording window over his data cuff.

Why the last one? Because his knack for survival is so ingrained in him that it sometimes transcends into pure instinct. Instinct says to get ready. So he's ready.

The stillness of Corn and Carrie, perhaps not knowing what they're seeing—or trying to unsee what can never be unseen—is too brief. Sebastian recognizes the instant when the truth of this moment sinks in for them. Though, who could miss it? It's like a switch has been flipped.

All the emotions they'd previously displayed fall away. Confusion, hurt, frustration, and maybe—a humongous maybe because Sebastian isn't convinced sludgebrains are really capable of it—affection. It all vanishes, leaving one raw emotion standing. Rage.

They erupt.

9

CORN AND CARRIE'S bodies bubble and tremor. They transform into creatures even more monster-y. Sebastian dives out of the way of flying claws and snapping fangs.

Buddy sheds its human appearance, limbs lengthening and muscles rippling as it scrabbles straight up the wall of rock.

Buddy wasn't wrong to boast of its speed. Corn and Carrie are fast, but Buddy is *fast*. By the time the two other sludgebrains reach for it, it's halfway up the cliff face.

The distance between the pursued and pursuers grows despite Corn and Carrie's best efforts. A lithe shadow highlighted by the silver of the moon, Buddy is almost to the precipice. If this is how fast it moves vertically, once it reaches flat terrain, there will be no catching it.

Corn must realize this because it opens its mouth and lets loose. Or Sebastian assumes it does. Again, he hears nothing. There's only the spike of the Dissonance. He hits Record on his holo-interface.

Then he decides to not waste the distraction Buddy has so generously provided. He dives for the lip of the ledge and flings himself over. The next ledge is halfway to the ground. He leaps just in time.

Carrie and Buddy, writhing from the pain of the shriek, fall—*THUD, THUD*—one after the other.

Sebastian throws himself against the cliff face as they continue to fall. They crash off the ledge he'd vacated mere seconds ago, then continue off the narrow strip he currently calls home. The two monsters smash to the ground below.

Something knocks into his back, sending him sprawling behind Carrie and Buddy. Instinctively, he curls to protect himself from the hard collision with the rocky ground. Lightning shoots up from his ankle.

Groaning, he rolls to pick himself up. A clawed fist wraps around his leg.

Ringu.

In all the excitement, he'd forgotten about the injured sludgebrain. Carrie had left it on the higher ledge during the mad dash to catch Buddy. That must have saved it from suffering the worst effects of the shriek. Otherwise, weak and injured as it is, Ringu wouldn't be moving right now.

Weak and injured or not, Ringu is still stronger than Sebastian. And hungry. Its grip is iron as it drags Sebastian toward it.

Sebastian reaches for the blaster that fell from his hand, but he's yanked away from it and even closer to Ringu.

The sludgebrain scrambles over Sebastian's legs, bulking up to use its mass to its favor. It presses its prey to the ground.

Sebastian can hardly move from the weight. Black hair spills over him like dark tangled webs. His hand twitches toward Tennille in his hip holster. He reaches instead for his holo-interface. Presses Play.

Ringu thrashes and rolls away.

Hardly believing that worked, Sebastian scrambles away from the tormented sludgebrain and reaches for Captain.

A giant hand swats it away. The blaster skids across the rocky ground, out of reach. Sebastian looks up and into the snarling maw of Children of the Corn. The sludgebrain towers over him, as colossal as any of the valley's stony monoliths.

"Filthy… human," it seethes. "Stealing shriek!"

"I really think your anger is misplaced," Sebastian says.

Corn lunges.

A blaster shot tears into its torso, sending it stumbling back. It bulks up even more—much to Sebastian's dismay because, seriously, how much bigger can this thing get before it's classified as a continent?

Children of the Corn charges forward.

Another shot comes, then another, and another, driving Corn back each time.

Meza steps into view from behind Sebastian. Her clothes are ripped, her hair lopsided, and her skin raw and broken. As she fires her Waster over and over, marching closer to the ever-more-feral sludgebrain, she's so cool and collected she could be folding laundry.

With a final blast, Corn collapses at last.

"Hey," Meza says.

"Hey," Sebastian breathes.

Corn doesn't move. Not so much as a twitch.

Sebastian grins at Meza. "You must feel like a BOSS right now."

How many other people can say they fell into a one-on-one brawl with a sludgebrain and came out the victor, as evidenced by the fact that she's here and Misery is not.

Then to come through like the cavalry and take out the final-level bad guy.

Meza shrugs. "Let's get out of here."

"Please and thank you."

After checking that his recording of Corn's powerful shriek is playing on repeat, Sebastian picks himself off the ground. And nearly falls right back on his face. A bolt of pain shoots up from his ankle.

When did that even happen?

The adrenaline of all that almost dying must have shielded him from the initial pain.

Gingerly, he puts a little weight on it. Twisted probably. Not broken.

He limps to his fallen Devastator and does a funny little balancing act to scoop it up while relying mostly on his right leg.

He takes in the prone sludgebrains scattered around them.

They lie limp in the dirt. The occasional stirring or moaning betrays that they're still alive. But they'll recover from this in no time and be right back to terrorizing any human unlucky enough to cross their path.

Even Corn, despite all the blaster fire hits, will probably make a full recovery. Given enough time.

Sludgebrains can bounce back from almost anything as long as their heads are intact. In all those shots, Meza hadn't once aimed for the head.

Sebastian remembers the promise she made to Buddy.

A promise that he himself did not make.

He levels Captain's barrel at Ringu's skull.

"Noooo…" Buddy croons weakly. It can barely lift its head. "Please."

"Don't worry. You ain't on the list. Even I ain't that unreasonable."

"Not killing… Hunters… Please…"

Sebastian keeps his blaster pointed right where it is but looks to Meza. "It does know that they just tried to kill it, right? And that they'll finish the job the second they're on their feet?"

"Please…" Buddy says. "F-Fa-family…"

"You know what?" Sebastian lifts his Devastator away from Ringu. "Your funeral."

He plans to be far, far away from these creatures by the time they're back on their feet. What happens to Buddy at that point is none of his business.

But then Meza is at Buddy's side, bending to prop its arms over her shoulder.

"C'mon," she shoots at Sebastian.

He doesn't move. "I'm confused. What's happening?"

"Gotta get Buddy to the bus."

Sebastian laughs.

Meza does not.

After a moment of absolute speechlessness, Sebastian limps to Buddy. "I can't believe I'm doing this."

Even with the two of them working together, it's a clumsy effort to move Buddy. Its bulk and long limbs slow them down as effectively as Sebastian's protesting ankle.

"You'd make this a ton easier if you could presto chango back to human size," Sebastian says through gritted teeth.

Buddy only groans, its head lolling to one side, then the other. It's completely out of it. Sebastian glances over his shoulder to make sure the other drones are just as down for the count.

Most are, but Carrie glares at them, mustering the strength to come after them. Its hands are braced against the ground as if to lift itself up. The movement takes visible effort, like gravity has doubled around it.

"Put it down," Meza says.

Sebastian happily complies. They let Buddy fall to its back on the ground. Sebastian nearly topples with it.

Meza kneels and takes its face in both her hands. "Buddy. Open your eyes. Look at me."

It drags its lids open.

"Change. Now."

It groans.

"This ain't a request."

Nothing happens at first, but then its form melts into that of a tall-but-scrawny teenage boy.

"Well, damn, Meza," Sebastian says in appreciation. Then he scrunches his face as he realizes something. When it comes to a contest of wills, he doesn't stand a chance against her, does he?

Moving Buddy becomes significantly easier after that, even with Sebastian being half-useless, thanks to his bum ankle.

They stop at the place where the cliff face gives way to the bridge.

"Kill me now," Sebastian says.

The steep, hill-like incline that gets them up to the bridge would be straightforward enough of a climb if Sebastian and Meza only had to worry about themselves.

Add a twisted ankle and an extra body to drag between them to the mix, and…

"We ain't gonna make it," Sebastian declares.

"I'll carry Buddy on my back."

"Have you forgotten that you're a head shorter than your friend here?"

She furrows her brows like it really had slipped her mind.

And maybe she really could carry the sludgebrain on her back. She is Meza, after all. But not up that sloping ground.

"Okay, here's what we're gonna do." Sebastian casts a glance back the way they came.

The fallen sludgebrains are dark lumps in the distance,

but they're still too close for comfort. And are they stirring? Kind of a lot?

With each step toward HRM, Sebastian carries the recording farther and farther from them. It continues to affect them but not as much as when he was right on them. But Buddy has been suffering the shriek looping almost directly into its ear.

"I'm shutting the recording off. You do your monster-whisperer thing and make Buddy help us get it up there. Fast."

She nods.

The moment Sebastian cuts the recording, the tension in Buddy's body eases. It sighs and slumps as if to slide to the ground. Which is not the result Sebastian had been hoping for.

"No," Meza says, tightening her arm around its waist. "You move, hear me? Or all this was for nothing. You move, or we all die."

Sebastian bites his tongue on the suggestion that they leave it behind, which would thus prevent the "we all die" scenario.

Together, he and Meza guide Buddy closer to the slope. They're still practically dragging it.

Down in the valley, one of those lumps is definitely doing more than stirring. Carrie is getting to its feet.

"Gonna let them take Scott from you?" Meza says.

Buddy attempts to lift its head, but its chin drops again. With a stifled groan, it takes a weak step forward, then another.

Meza nods toward Sebastian. "I got this. Worry about getting yourself up there."

Sebastian pulls out from under Buddy's arm. It carries its own weight. Sort of. Meza remains at its side to steady it.

In the valley, Carrie is shuffling forward. Weakly at first, but each step is more sure than the last.

Cursing his ankle, the slope, and every jutting rock he trips over, Sebastian climbs. Meza remains remarkably neutral about the dirty, naked monster boy pressed against her. So Sebastian does his best to be cool about his view from behind.

He's huffing and puffing by the time they clamber onto the bridge, but that's mostly due to his ankle making the short hike harder than it had to be.

He spares a glance into the valley.

"Run," he says. "Run, run, run!"

Because Carrie sure is. Not as fast as it moved before, but that's hardly a reason to breathe easy.

He considers hitting Play on the recording, but Buddy has also grown steadier without the shriek on loop, and HRM is so close now, much closer than Carrie is to them, and Sebastian's ankle is killing him, and if he has to drag that sludgebrain any farther, his foot just might snap off.

Sebastian runs as fast as he can limp.

Ahead of him, Meza's hand reaches for HRM's back door. A scraping sound comes from behind him. Carrie is dragging itself over the bridge's rail. Meza flings open the door. Carrie propels itself at its prey.

Sebastian hits Play.

Both sludgebrains collapse in agony.

Sebastian allows himself a single breath of relief before limping the rest of the way to HRM.

After dragging Buddy onto the bus, Sebastian stumbles over the body dumped unceremoniously in the aisle. Let Meza make sure it's nice and comfy. He doesn't care much.

He only has eyes for the driver's seat.

The current generators purr as HRM starts up. It's the loveliest sound Sebastian has ever heard.

Truly.

Johann Sebastian Bach would weep to hear such magic. Wolfgang Amadeus Mozart couldn't have penned a more beautiful symphony had he a hundred years to try. Ludwig van Beethoven would take an ax to his piano and chop it into a million pieces from the despair that comes with the knowledge that he couldn't begin to compare his work to that angelic sound.

Seconds later, Sebastian, Meza, and the weeping ghosts of various, long-dead composers are tearing down the road and away from the pack of vicious, unholy monsters.

Well, except for the one they're carrying with them.

But Sebastian isn't quite ready to wrap his brain around that little development.

10

THE MOONLIT BEHEMOTHS HUGGING the road fly by in a blur. Sebastian swings around bends in the road at less-than-safe speeds.

Considering the state in which they left those sludgebrains, thanks to the recorded shriek and—in the case of Children of the Corn—Meza's Waster, there's no way the monsters can give chase. Even so, Sebastian can't get out of the valley fast enough.

"Buddy's in pain," Meza calls from the back of HRM. "Switch off that recording."

Sebastian hesitates, considers that it might be best for a sludgebrain in such close proximity to remain incapacitated. Sure, it had sort of helped save his and Meza's lives. But a sludgebrain is still a sludgebrain.

With a shake of his head at his own stupidity, he glances at his data cuff to turn off the looping shriek.

Meza sinks into the passenger seat a moment later. Finger on the trigger of her Waster, she scowls at the shadowed giants passing outside her window.

"Don't think they're usually exposed to that sound so long," she says, "but I reckon Buddy's okay now."

"Oh, goody," Sebastian says.

"That recording. We gotta share it. Gonna change things in the Midlands."

"Sebastian Yun does it again!" He holds up his holo-interface to bask in the glory of his achievement. "My legend will live on for—"

He clears his throat and flicks the screen off.

"What?" Meza asks.

"Nothing."

"Something."

"So like… what if there ain't actually a recording to share? I mean, everybody done got by without it all this time."

She doesn't say anything. Sebastian keeps his eyes on the road.

"You didn't save the recording," she says.

"I mean, a lot's been going on tonight. A bunch of heart-stopping, near-death experiences, winning against incredible odds, and general kicking of monster ass. No one's at fault, really. And I want you to know, I don't blame you. Anyone coulda hit the delete button instead of Save."

"And when your data cuff asked you to confirm the delete?"

"It ain't a big deal. I'm sure we'll have ample opportunity to record another super-powerful sludgebrain shriek in a frequency humans cannot perceive with the naked ear. And speaking of naked, that was a whole lotta nudity, right? And wasn't none of it a sexy good time."

"Sebastian." Her voice is full of recrimination.

"So anyway… Back to cataloging all the reasons you can't live without me."

"Gotta be kidding me."

"Maybe?"

"Always been so needy," she says, "or this a learned trait?"

"We may never know."

"Just drive."

"Yes, ma'am."

Sebastian drives. And drives and drives. Even after the last of the rock formations disappears from the rear camera feeds, he puts hours and the night between them and that sinister valley. Meza remains quiet but vigilant at his side.

He drives until he's too exhausted to keep going. He'd like to put even more distance between him and those sludge-brains, but him being behind the wheel is quickly becoming a bad idea.

Besides, there are things that must be seen to.

One thing in particular.

Buddy hadn't said one word the entire time they drove. Some might even say its silence is suspicious, as if it hoped Sebastian would forget it had been brought aboard. As if he could forget.

They've come to a stop on a long stretch of open road with wide views on all sides. Sebastian twists in his seat to verify that, yes, indeed he did bring a monster into his place of refuge and serenity. It had not been a hysteria-induced hallucination.

Buddy sits in the aisle, in the section of the lower deck Sebastian has dubbed the entertainment lounge. Slumped against the couch with its knees drawn up, it buries its head in its arms.

"Sebastian…" Meza says, anticipating his next words.

"It can't stay."

"It's all alone."

"It eats humans." Sebastian points to himself and Meza to remind her of their place on this food chain.

"We are not having to eat humans," Buddy says quietly.

It lifts its head to meet Sebastian's eyes. Never has anyone looked so lost. Sebastian turns away.

Meza crosses her arms. "It took a huge risk trying to save us. Nearly got killed for it. Those other sludgebrains won't keep their mouths shut about what happened back there. Buddy ain't got a home no more."

"That don't mean it's sticking around here. Though, I absolutely wish you the best." Sebastian gives Buddy a two-fingered salute. "It saved our lives, and we saved it right back. That makes us square in my book."

"You don't believe that."

"I believe it's a really dumb idea to have that thing creeping around when we're sleeping or have our backs turned or any time we let our guards down. You can't be okay with carrying a monster into every town that opens its gates for us. People trust us, Meza."

"And I trust Buddy."

"Still no. A hard no. A no that encompasses all the nos that have been or ever will be." Then, specifically to make sure he's being absolutely clear, he sings in a rich, silky baritone, "Hell nooo. Nooo. Nooo. No no. No no. Wait, it's about to get to the good part." Plugging one ear with his finger, he digs deep for the next set of runs. "Nooo noooooo nononon—"

"Fine. I'll go with it."

"What?"

"You're right," she says. "I believe it's trying to do better. That ain't no guarantee it's safe. You shouldn't have to risk your life for something you don't believe in. You go on your way. Me and Buddy'll go ours."

"Whoa. Hold up." Sebastian raises his palms as if to slow down the moment. His brain can't quite seem to catch up to this turn. "Where's all this coming from anyway? This whole sentimental, take-a-chance-on-a-monster thing ain't you."

"Maybe you don't know me."

Sebastian bites his lips, thinking. He wants to rebut that statement but struggles to justify a counterargument.

Has it really been only months that they've been traveling together? Not years?

"Maybe I don't," he admits.

Somehow, he keeps forgetting that, in the grand scheme of things, their acquaintance with each other has been a short one.

"Never planned to start traveling together," Meza says. "Just sorta happened. Neither of us expected this to last forever. So today's the day we part ways. You'll go back to traveling alone, and you'll be okay. Because you're always okay. I'll take the risk of being a friend to someone who needs it."

"But…"

"But what?"

"But… I—You…"

Nothing she'd said was wrong. Not like he needs her to stay. As she pointed out, he doesn't need anyone. He'll get by. Same as he used to.

Even if having another person around has been nice, it doesn't have to be Meza. There are other people in the world. Plenty of them are good with tech and know how to point a blaster. He can let her go.

"You're going about this in the entirely wrong way," he says. "We both know there's only one way to solve this. If you win, the monster of unspeakable evil can stay."

When her rock loses to his dagger, she shrugs as if this were all inevitable, hops out of the passenger's seat, and starts up the aisle.

"Gotta decide how much of our salvages and refurbs are mine. Need something to trade for a ride when we reach the next town."

"Wait!" He catches the end of her jacket and draws her back to him. "Two out of three."

Sebastian loses. Twice.

Maybe she noticed that he was a little delayed in the third round when he threw out a dagger that was defeated by her blaster.

Maybe she didn't.

Maybe it's one of those things that doesn't need to be commented upon.

He lets out a long, tired sigh and stares at Meza over the decisive finger game hanging between them.

His brain must be scrambled from lack of sleep and all of tonight's life-and-death shenanigans. He's really going along with this.

But she's not going anywhere. Not today anyway.

"First things first. Instruct your new pet here how to use the shower. And find it some clothes."

He grimaces, realizing it's going to be his clothes.

Meza must be in a good mood. She doesn't throw him a dirty look for issuing her commands. Crouching next to Buddy, she places a hand on its bare shoulder.

"C'mon," she says. "Follow me."

She leads it to the top deck.

Sebastian's ankle throbs, reminding him it's well overdue for some TLC. Or, at the very least, a bit of basic first aid.

He limps down the aisle and yanks open the cabinet holding their sad excuse for medical supplies. After plopping down on the couch, he winces as he carefully and so, so slowly removes his boot then his sock.

"Ain't you a beaut," he sings at the swollen, purpled skin.

While wrapping his ankle snuggly with strips of cloth, he dispassionately examines his most recent actions.

Why had he insisted on keeping Meza around, even

though she's now apparently a packaged deal with that sludgebrain?

It's not that he suddenly needs people—or Meza in particular. Never that.

But he can admit that having someone else around hasn't been bad. And it might as well be someone who's a genius at fixing things and has unerring aim with a blaster. And who would strike a deal with a monster to bring him back from a pit of darkness.

Yup. That's it. Basic companionship and utility.

He is *not* getting attached.

Sense of self salvaged, he considers the small vial of painkiller. The stuff is expensive, and the liquid is getting perilously low. He and Meza try not to use it unless absolutely needed.

He decides that he's earned it and squeezes two drops onto his tongue.

Sebastian's waiting at the bottom of the narrow, spiral staircase when Meza climbs back down, alone. Arms crossed and brows knit, he leans against the frame to keep his weight off the freshly wrapped foot.

"I ain't sure about this," he says. "Like. At all."

She leans against the stairwell frame opposite him, hand propped on her hip. "I am."

He gives a heavy sigh. His gaze flickers toward the second level where a freakin' sludgebrain is using his shower, putting on his clothes, and is generally way too close to where he lays his head at night.

"I guess that'll have to be good enough for me. Until, you know, it murders us in our sleep. At which point my ghost will introduce your ghost to the 'I Told You So' song. It's part two of the sensational, chart-topping 'No' song."

"It'll be fine. They're good guys. Both of them."

"Mm," Sebastian grunts. Neither an agreement nor a rebuttal. At best, it's a lazy *"We'll see."*

The entrance to the stairs is narrow. Leaning against either side, Sebastian and Meza are within arm's reach of each other. Closer. They linger there, as if both sensing that there's more needing to be said.

Her gaze wanders away from his. "Wasn't just mad about you getting us in trouble. I know how to take care of myself, even in the wake of your idiocy. Want you to care about what happens to you, is all."

"I care."

"Don't act like it."

"Well…" Sebastian tries to pull up a counterargument but fails to grasp one.

It's not that he doesn't care about his well-being. Not exactly. But he knows it's a slim chance he'll die an old man or peacefully in his sleep. Not with things on this planet being the way they are.

He can't let something as written in the stars as his early demise stop him from living.

"You—What you do—" Meza bites her lip. Again, she can't quite seem to look right at him. Her eyes find his chest instead of his face.

Sebastian waits. She tries again.

"Your show's about more than music. You're doing something different. Something… special. Get yourself killed, *So You Survived the End of the World* would be over."

Finally, her eyes meet his. It's a simple, honest gaze, and yet Sebastian wouldn't be able to look away if he tried.

"It would be too soon."

Sebastian's lips curl into a slow, sleepy grin. "Meza. Are you saying I'm irreplaceable?"

That look of openness slams shut. "Never mind. Forget I said anything."

She spins away from him and marches up the aisle.

"What? No! Come back. I'm sure you got more to say on the topic of how awesome I am. You didn't even get to my charismatic smile or trendsetting style."

"Bite me, Sebastian."

"I'm serious!" He limps after her, leaning against the driver's seat when she takes the wheel. "Remember a bunch of months ago when I started wearing fingerless gloves, then everybody started wearing fingerless gloves? Then I had to stop wearing them because they weren't cool no more?"

She doesn't respond. Other than shooting him a look that says he's an idiot.

When she punches the button to start HRM, the engine hums to life beautifully. What would Sebastian do if he had to go back to fixing all the things that broke on this rig by himself? He'd get it done, of course, but not as quickly and efficiently as her.

"I call it the Bazzy Affect," he continues. "And you're right. This world cannot be deprived of that."

"I take it back. Be a moron. Send yourself to an early grave, for all I care."

Impulsively, and maybe riding the residual high of surviving the night, he reaches forward and grabs her hand. She stills.

"I'll try to be more careful."

"Okay," she says quietly, and, for a whole three seconds, lets his hand lay on top of hers. Then she clears her throat and slips her hand free.

"I make no promises though." Sebastian falls into the passenger seat and lifts his injured foot onto the dashboard. Best to keep it elevated and all. "It's difficult to contain this much pure awesome."

"Sure. That's your problem."

He disregards her sardonicism.

She's already said that he's an astoundingly amazing person and the world doesn't deserve him.

Exact quote. No take-backsies.

Activating his holo-interface, Sebastian hits the broadcast button and switches on his mic. Might not be many people out there listening at this time of night, but that's okay.

"I apologize for earlier's abrupt interruption, my loyal listeners," he says. "You know how it is. Sometimes these situations pop up, and they got a way of running away from you. And, boy howdy, did this one get weird. I'll tell y'all about it one day. Maybe."

Sebastian shakes his head. Not quite believing who—what—they've brought aboard HRM. Or his part in it.

"I been inspired to give you insomniacs some Jay-Z to get you through the night. 'Cuz I got ninety-nine problems, but the—"

A quick glance at Meza makes it clear that finishing that sentence would not be wise.

"Well, you know how the rest goes. Anyhoo, in case you were worried about me and Meza, you can breathe easy now. We're just fine."

THE STORY BEHIND THE STORY

Sometimes, there's this magical moment as an author when you finish a first draft and you know it's amazing.

The best thing since sliced bread. The height of artistic expression. The Taj Mahal of brilliant storytelling.

That was the feeling I had when I completed the first draft for this book.

My goal at the time was to complete the first drafts for the first four books in this series as quickly as possible. So once I finished the draft, I set it aside and got to work on writing the next in series.

It was probably a year later when I returned to my first draft of this novella. I opened the file with much anticipation—remembering with delight how superb it was—and started reading.

And.

It.

Was.

Terrible.

Seriously, reading it was almost painful.

It was a "burn it all down and rebuild from scratch" sort

of awful. Other than the first and final scene, everything had to go!

After a mourning period, I pulled up my sleeves and got to work. Because my characters deserved better.

I spent a lot of time thinking about how to write my body-snatching monsters.

They aren't mindless killing machines, and that was the real challenge. These are thinking, reasoning creatures who make the choice to enslave other conscious beings. Which is heinous. But while these sludgebrains would be absolutely monstrous, I also needed them to have genuine bonds with each other.

I wrote out questions that explored who the slugdebrains are—both as a society and as individuals members of the hunting party— and I forced myself to be thorough in answering them. I asked myself what daily life has been like for Scott, what Buddy's history is with the other hunters, what strategies do sludgebrains use when hunting humans, and so on.

Fun fact about me: I hate pre-writing exercises. You know, the list of 5,001 random character questions like "What's their favorite color?" and "Do they have a birthmark?"

But I'll give credit where it's due. It can be a pretty dang useful exercise.

Interviewing my characters and asking myself questions helped me see Buddy and the other sludgebrains as complex beings with their own customs, values, and views on their place in the world. It made the dynamic between Buddy and the other hunters much more specific. Each of the other hunters were given their own outlooks, temperaments, and motivations.

Suddenly one of the sludgebrains became a Sebastian superfan—the unhealthy kind. And if humans can get scary when their fanaticism goes too far, how much worse is it when that scarily obsessed fan is a body-snatching monster?

Thus, Ringu sprang to life, demanded to be an integral part of the story, and it led to some deliciously creepy moments in my *a-hem* lighthearted and delightful post-apoc novella.

Ringu is also the reason a good chunk of this story takes place in a cave.

While working out those cave scenes, I drew on my own experiences touring a system of caves.

Fun fact #2! Both of my parents are from Kentucky. It's where I have spent many a summer in my younger years.

But it wasn't until I was well into adulthood that I had the thought that maybe I should do things other than laying around various relatives' houses. Perhaps I should learn about and take advantage of the historical and cultural sights worth seeing around those parts.

One of the places I decided to visit was Mammoth Cave, which is the longest cave system known to the world. No, I didn't pull that from memory. I had to look it up.

The excellent tour guide shared a myriad of stories about the cave's history, not all of it pleasant. One of my favorite parts of the tour was when our guide brought us to a huge cavern, instructed us to remain absolutely quiet for a few seconds, and turned out the lights.

It was the kind of darkness that was so complete, it was way too easy to forget that you were standing inches from a bunch of other people.

It was unforgettable, and the sort of experience that sends the imagination down all sorts of rabbit holes.

And very useful for when, a couple years later, one decides to—I don't know—write a little something about a guy who gets dragged into unfathomable depths by a creature of unspeakable evil.

Choosing to throw out an entire draft is never an easy decision, but I'm super glad I did it. I'm pleased as punch with what I was able to give you in the final version of this book.

K.C. Cordell
    California, August 2024

WHAT'S NEXT? POST-APOCALYPTIC DJ: BOOK 2!

GRAB THE NEXT BOOK NOW AT
WWW.KCCORDELL.COM/BOOKS

Here's your sneak peak at Sebastian, Meza and Scott Buddy's next adventure: ***So You Want to Rob the Bandit Queen (Post-Apocalyptic DJ: Book 2)***

Beneath the unrelenting glare of the sun, Sebastian, Meza, and Scott Buddy have positioned themselves in a small cluster of rock formations. They lay side by side on top of a big ol' boulder, flat on their bellies and squinting at the bandit stronghold in the distance.

Correction. Sebastian is squinting. Meza is hogging the binoculars.

He taps her arm incessantly. "Lemme see. It's my turn already!"

"Wouldn't have to borrow mine if you hadn't lost yours," she says coolly. Not so much as a muscle twitches to hand over the binoculars. Her hair, often a dark, textured cloud haloing her head, has been sleeked down into thick braids running along her skull.

"I did not lose them," Sebastian says. "I just… Look, I had a ton of planning to see to and a short amount of time in which to do it. Excuse me for forgetting to pack my binoculars when I was hard at work, seeing to all the various details."

"Going shopping so you can play dress-up, you mean."

"That was a vital part of the plan!"

"Cloud is looking like fluffy bird."

Correction number two. Sebastian is squinting at the bandit stronghold in the distance. Meza is hogging the binoculars. And Scott Buddy, on Sebastian's left, is stretched out on its back, staring at the lone cloud drifting across the desolate sky and, apparently, imagining its next meal.

Sebastian ignores its comment, tries to ignore his uncomfortable proximity to the thing beside him altogether.

"Don't be a meanie," he tells Meza. "Sharing is caring. I need to see what's going on down there too."

"When I'm done," she says.

"Share Bear would be so disappointed in your behavior right now."

"Am I supposed to know what a Share Bear is?"

"All the cool kids do." Sebastian shrugs and returns his attention to the huge structure sitting on the horizon. "I'll let you figure out what it means that you don't."

To be fair, he might be the only person in the entire broken world who knows anything about Care Bears. Nobody spends as much time as he does surfing the data streams of the past, fishing up old shows, movies, books, and —of course—music.

This encyclopedic knowledge of pop culture from centuries long past is sure to come in handy as they attempt today's impossible task of sneaking into an enormous, dicey bandit stronghold. If anyone has an appreciation for long-dead pop culture, it'll be the cutthroats packed into the den of iniquity below.

Right. And hellions make adorable house pets.

"Is it just me," Sebastian says, "or are there a lot more bad guys here than there oughta be? I know the Black Ravens are the biggest crew of them all, but this here's a lot, right?"

The ridge from which he and Meza observe provides the perfect vantage for scoping out the infamous Desperado City, home base for the largest, most intense crew of bandits out there.

Because, of course, bandits are a thing. As if the hordes of hellish creatures and body-snatching monsters preying on humanity aren't enough. At least most Midlanders don't have enough of anything to be worth most bandits' time. It's those poor rich Feudlanders to the south, with their fertile farms and fancy knickknacks, who suffer from the bulk of the bandits' attention.

As if to prove they're bigger and badder than everyone else, this crew is holed up in some sort of humongous warehouse left over from the days when everyone used to live in automated cities that made everyday life unbelievably easy. Humanity thought they'd built themselves a utopia. At least until those cities turned against their masters. It was the beginning of a worldwide nightmare that's still felt generations later.

Understandably, folks have been giving technology the side-eye since then. Most only make use of what they absolutely must for survival. And even though the AI that ran every aspect of life in the old cities had been disabled generations ago, no one wants to live in the shells of what once was. Call it a healthy dose of paranoia.

But bandits are not generally known for making the best life choices.

The enormous warehouse sits on the near horizon like a blocky mountain presiding over the surrounding wasteland. It's massive. More than a few towns—or settlements—Sebastian has visited could fit inside there all at once. The front of the building is emblazoned with a giant black raven encircled with thorns. It's the mark of the crew that claims this territory.

Meza grunts an agreement in response to Sebastian's question. "More than Black Raven marks on them rides."

Finally, she hands over the binoculars. Sebastian peers through them and focuses on the painted details of the vehicles crowded around the building. "Is that—?"

"The Wild Raiders' mark." Meza confirms what Sebastian's eyes are telling him.

Parked haphazardly all around the massive building are hundreds and hundreds of those distinctive bandit vehicles. The black-and-red trucks, motorcycles, and ATVs are adorned with demon horns, bloody fangs, and rotting skulls —both real and painted.

Bandits pimp out their rides with one goal in mind: scare the living ghost out of anyone who spots them as they emerge, roaring, from a furious dirt cloud on the horizon.

A large swath of vehicles share the same symbol. A screaming skull engulfed in flames. Some painted sloppily. Some stenciled. Each of them mean the same thing—the second biggest bandit crew is in attendance.

"What's going on down there?" Sebastian says. "Black Ravens and Wild Raiders hate each other. They can't cross each other's territory without all hell breaking loose."

"Look over there." Meza pushes the binoculars in a new direction.

"Those are—"

"Bashers."

Their mark—a big wooden bat with barbed wire wrapped around it—announces their presence as clear as day.

"Well, ain't that fun," Sebastian says. "It would appear that they are having a little shindig. So now, instead of just one, we gotta sneak into a place filled with the three biggest crews in all of existence. I'm so glad we decided to steal a valuable piece of Old World tech from bandits today."

"You decided to steal from bandits," Meza says. "You. The endless source of insane ideas."

"Not all crazy ideas come outta my head." To make it clear exactly what he means, Sebastian sends a significant look to his left.

And turns just in time to see Scott Buddy ripping a bloody mouthful out of a fat buzzard. The splatters of blood sizzle on the rocky sun-heated surface between them.

Sebastian twists away. "Oh, gross. It's doing it again!"

"Leave them alone," Meza says. "They gotta eat. Just like everybody else."

"It's eating all the time. With its mouth open right in my face."

Scrunching his nose at the pool of blood inching toward him, Sebastian makes the short jump from his perch. He lands in the shade of the surrounding boulders.

"Somebody coulda warned me I'd have a front-row seat to the most disgusting show on earth when I agreed to your crazy idea of harboring a freakin' man-eating, body-snatching creature of evil. Ow!" He rubs the stinging spot on his shoulder where Meza has just kicked him.

She glares down. "They ain't evil. Not either one of them. You'd better stop calling them that."

"Why ain't you ever that nice to me, Meza?"

She rolls her eyes down to Sebastian. "You look ridiculous." All notes of warmth and kindness have left her voice.

"See. That there is exactly what I'm talking about. And I look like a badass."

"You mean a jackass?"

Scott chuckles.

"I meant what I said, woman."

"Can you even move in them pants?"

Sebastian's ensemble can be summed up in two words.

Black leather.

Because everybody—except Meza, apparently—knows that black leather is the very height of bandit couture. They probably don't even know that other materials and colors exist. So Sebastian isn't taking any chances. Boots, pants, shirt, jacket. He's literally got this covered.

Although, he'd had to pull his ensemble together on short notice, so some compromises were made. Not like he had time to shop around. The black leather jacket he managed to barter for has fringe dangling all along the inseams of the sleeves. Not exactly in step with his personal brand, but he's decided he likes it.

The shirt… well, it's more of a man's crop top. Like, super cropped. Like, did they run out of material, and that's why it barely comes past his nipples? But he's pretty sure he's seen bandit dudes in shirts like this before. Plus, with the strap of his Devastator's holster across his chest, it sorta comes together just right.

Besides, he's totally ripped and owes it to the world to show off his hot bod more often. And if he's being honest, the pale skin of his torso could use the opportunity to catch up with his tanned face and arms.

Sure, the pants are just a teeny bit tighter than he'd prefer, but again, short notice. He did pretty good, considering.

"As always," Sebastian says, "I move with the grace and precision of a panther stalking its prey."

Meza stares at him in a way that tells him he's an idiot without her having to say the words.

"At least I made an effort," he says. "Even Scott Buddy put on the vest I found for it."

"I am also looking like badass." Scott straightens the studded black vest it wears, smudging bloody fingerprints across the fabric, but where they're all going, that'll probably help sell the look.

Sebastian gestures toward Meza, looking just normal in the same sort of thing she always wears. Just-normal mechanic coveralls over just-normal shirts and shorts. The top half of her coveralls is currently tied around her waist by the sleeves. "You call that a disguise?"

"Call it not dressing like an idiot."

"Have you ever even seen a bandit? I'm telling you, this is how they dress."

"You got a gallon of sweat dripping off you."

Sebastian stops himself from wiping at the deluge collecting on his brow. Admittedly, heavy, unbreathable leather is not the best material with which to plaster oneself in sweltering heat.

"Here's how it's gonna go down." He snatches his messenger bag from where he'd plopped it onto the ground and tosses the strap over his head. "We sneak into Desperado City. Me and Scott Buddy successfully blend in 'cuz we are totally pulling off these looks, but then you get us caught 'cuz you ain't put on that black strappy number I picked out for you."

"Gonna faint from heatstroke before any of that happens," she says flatly.

"Whatever. Let's get this over with. Upon further consideration, I reckon this whole bandit-convention thing is gonna work to our advantage. Sneaking in there will be a breeze. And since my disguise is flawless, I'll pretend to be the new guy learning the ropes, which will allow me to casually ask a few questions about how things work around here. I'll get my Sherlock on and figure out where they keep the good stuff. Then we grab that gorgeous arm and get out before anyone even notices it's missing. Easy peasy."

So You Want to Rob the Bandit Queen (Post-Apocalyptic DJ: Book 2)

READ IT TODAY!

www.kccordell.com/books

SOMETHING AWESOME JUST FOR YOU!

Psst… Psst! Yeah, you! Want a free book?

Maybe you're craving more…

- Super fun, loveable characters
- That quirky humor you now know and love
- Larger-than-life monster action

Get your hands on K.C. Cordell's epic fantasy novella, *Destroying a World Eater for Beginners* for abso-freakin-lutely FREE when you sign up for her Newsletter of Awesomeness!

Visit:
www.kccordell.com/newsletter
and start reading today!

A WEIRDO HAS ABDUCTED YARI TO HIS CREEPY LAIR AND
EXPECTS HER TO DO WHAT?!

SAVE THE WORLD, YOU PERV. GET YOUR HEAD OUT OF
THE GUTTER AND START READING

Yari of Inera is a nobody. No. She's less than that. A mouthy orphan who gets by on her street smarts and nimble feet, she knows her place. So when she's plucked from her ordinary life and brought to an eerie, colorless fortress to be told by a man on a throne that she's some chosen one, she isn't impressed. She's seen her share of grifts and tricks. This one's no different.

Only her abductor's tricks defy her best attempts to explain them away. But stubborn to a fault, Yari will require solid evidence before she believes anything this strange man says about a world eater coming to destroy the planet. Or her being the one to stop it

Unfortunately for her, irrefutable proof is exactly what her abductor has in mind. Even if it puts her directly in the path of a cataclysmic disaster that she is nowhere near ready to take on...

If you like surly mentors, smart-mouthed chosen ones, and big monsters with even bigger appetites, then this gripping action and adventure fantasy is right up your alley!

www.kccordell.com/newsletter

THE WIND BENEATH MY WINGS

Special thanks to my family. Somehow you guys still tolerate me. Which might be up there somewhere between splitting the Red Sea and getting a final *Game of Thrones* book, as far as miraculous events go.

To my readers: Willie, Abigail, Richard, Odessa, and Zoe. I appreciate you being the first to read this book. It's super cool of you to let me believe that I might know what I'm doing.

To Jay, Cherise, and Willie (again), and to the Queens of the Quill: It's an honor and pleasure to be in the trenches with you.

Thank you, Rashida, Darlene, and Brittany of Red Adept Editing and Nicole of Proof Before You Publish, for helping me give this book the ol' spitshine and polish. Let the record show that they did their best to stop me from breaking the English language too much. For all incidents of poetic grammar usage found within this book, blame me. And, also, those poetry classes I was forced to take in college. Everything is always poetry's fault...

To you, dear reader: Thanks for picking up this book and making it all the way through to the acknowledgements. You're a superstar!

And a final thanks to K.A. Applegate. Because who knows if body snatchers would have made it into this book if not for a certain alien invasion series I obsessed over as a young, budding writer.

BTDUBS... WHO WROTE THIS BOOK ANYWAY?

L.A. native K.C. Cordell likes writing about aliens, monsters and superpowers. She attempted to write her first novel when she was nine. She didn't finish it, but it's still floating around. She read it recently. It's pretty good.

She likes reading and watching junk about aliens, monsters and superpowers too. Some of her favorite books and shows from growing up in the '90s include *Animorphs, Ella Enchanted, Gargoyles, Spiderman: The Animated Series,* and *Buffy the Vampire Slayer.* These inspired her to pick up a pen and their influence can still be seen in the writing she does today.

She hopes to one day own a t-shirt with an alpaca wearing an afro on it. If she ever got a puppy, she would name him Kiba. Thanks to once upon a time reading many, MANY books on the topic to her nephew, she's pretty good at pronouncing dinosaur names. Her favorite to say is pachycephalosaurus.

"Pachycephalosaurus."

Nice!

But she totally has to look up how to spell it.

Connect with K.C. on TikTok:
@bykccordell

www.ingramcontent.com/pod-product-compliance
Lightning Source LLC
Chambersburg PA
CBHW031054310726
48969CB00007B/2273